Pecos
Crossing

Pecos
Crossing

Elmer Kelton

A TOM DOHERTY ASSOCIATES BOOK
NEW YORK

This is a work of fiction. All of the characters, organizations, and events portrayed in this novel are either products of the author's imagination or are used fictitiously.

PECOS CROSSING

Copyright © 1963 by Elmer Kelton

Pecos Crossing was originally published in 1963 by Ballantine Books as *Horsehead Crossing* and first published by Forge Books in 2007, in the Elmer Kelton omnibus *Texas Showdown*.

A Forge Book
Published by Tom Doherty Associates, LLC
175 Fifth Avenue
New York, NY 10010

www.tor-forge.com

Forge® is a registered trademark of Tom Doherty Associates, LLC.

ISBN-13: 978-0-7653-4895-1
ISBN-10: 0-7653-4895-0

First Edition: June 2008

Printed in the United States of America

0 9 8 7 6 5 4 3 2 1

Pecos
Crossing

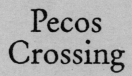

I

In the 1890s a mile was a distance that a man could respect. From Sonora, Texas, up to San Angelo, and from there west to the Pecos River was a long, rough, dangerous trail, especially when a man paused every so often and turned in the saddle to look back with worried eyes for someone who might be following. . . .

A lot of Texas maps didn't even show Sonora, for scarcely more than a decade had passed since it first began as a trading post on the San Antonio-El Paso Road. Much of it was fresh and new, the unpainted lumber not yet blistered and darkened in the sun. But to Johnny Fristo and Speck Quitman, riding in after spending the winter in a cow camp far down on the Devil's River, it wouldn't have mattered if Sonora had been a hundred years old. It was there, and so were they. A long winter had bowed out to spring, and this was going to be payday.

Speck was as eager as a new-weaned pup loosed on a fresh scent. "She's a peach of a town, ain't she, Johnny? Didn't seem this pretty when we left here last fall."

Johnny Fristo made a more sober appraisal of the scattered frame buildings and Mexican adobes huddled in open sunshine between the rough limestone hills along the river's dry fork. "No town looks like much when you're ridin' out of it with your pockets emptied."

For that matter, they weren't bringing much back. All these cowboys owned, they carried on their horses. Tied behind the high cantle of each saddle was a yellow

Fish Brand slicker, a wool blanket and a warbag, bulging with their "thirty years' gatherings." The latter was a misnomer because neither had lived thirty years yet. Johnny was twenty-two and admitted it. Speck was the same and claimed twenty-five.

They had had a run of luck last fall, both good and bad. They had worked all summer with a wagon crew gathering cattle from the rocky hills and the liveoak thickets of the broad Edwards Plateau. After fall branding, the boss paid them off. They drifted into Sonora hoping to find something else. They hadn't found work, but the chuckleheaded Speck had found a man who was willing to teach him about poker. The lessons came high. By the time Johnny Fristo found out Speck had lost all their money, the "teacher" had vanished, bound for San Angelo and points north. The cowboys would have spent the winter swamping out saloons and sleeping on a porch if a hawk-faced cow trader named Larramore hadn't shown up. Larramore was looking for somebody to work cheap and take care of a steer herd he planned to winter down on the river. He was paying pasturage to Old Man Hoskins, who had more grass than he was using. Johnny and Speck spent the winter in a picket shack that was really half dugout, pitifully short of coffee and tobacco but a healthy distance from all temptation.

A few days ago a worried-looking Larramore had ridden into camp with a couple of extra men to gather the steers. He lamented that the cattle market had gone as sour as last week's milk, but he had finally managed to find a buyer.

"You fellers stay and patch up for Old Man Hoskins," Larramore said as he drove the cattle away. "I'll meet you in Sonora Friday and pay you off."

Luckily for Johnny and Speck, the good-natured

old rancher had come by the camp. "Forget about patchin' up," he had said. "You punchers have coyoted out here all winter. Go git yourselves a taste of civilization. And drink one for *me*."

Now Speck licked dry lips and glanced toward the first saloon. "Larramore'll be real surprised. Reckon he's got the money for them cattle yet?"

Johnny nodded. "I expect so. Shouldn't make him any difference whether he pays us today or pays us Friday. Comes to the same figure anyhow."

They were a contrasting pair, not much alike except in age. Folks usually took a liking to the swivel-jawed Speck. He talked all the time, though sometimes he got so carried away that his talk quit making sense. Speck was short and bandy-legged, with a round face and freckles. His hair was rusty, his eyes a laughing blue. He could ride any bronc they led out to him and could rope anything that would run. Some folks said Speck had probably been sitting on a fence telling a windy when the Lord was passing out brains. At any rate, he hadn't quite gotten his share. If occasionally some rancher flared up and fired Speck for the tomfool stunts he pulled, he was likely to hire him back in a day or two. He was a good cowboy. A man could put up with a little flightiness.

Another reason ranchmen tolerated Speck's shenanigans was because they had to take Speck if they wanted Johnny Fristo. When you hired one, you hired both. When you fired Speck, Johnny went too.

Johnny didn't often have much to say. With Speck around, he didn't get much chance to talk anyway, and he had long since quit trying. Johnny was taller, thinner of build. He didn't share Speck's flashy ways, but he was always around to help pull his partner out of a jackpot. Johnny would be out doing his job with a quiet competence while Speck was still talking about it. He could ride along with his gaze on the horizon, his mind a hundred miles away, nod agreement to everything Speck said and not actually hear a word of it.

They had spent their boyhoods in the Concho River country up around the army post and cow town of San Angelo, sixty-five miles north of Sonora. Johnny's father raised cattle on a small ranch back from the North Concho. Speck had been brought up in San Angelo by an aunt till he was about fourteen. Then he had landed a job as a horse jingler out on Spring Creek. Once or twice a year Speck worked up courage to make a duty call to his aunt. He would get away as quickly as he could.

"She's a sweet old lady," Johnny had heard him say with a certain reverence. "But she's mean as hell."

Today they came into Sonora by way of the Del Rio road. Eastward, halfway up a hill, stood the new Sutton County courthouse. Horses lazed at hitching racks and posts along the sloping, dusty street. Sweating freighters grunted at the weight as they unloaded store goods from a heavy wagon that had hauled them down from the railroad in San Angelo. A pair of smaller wagons, one tied behind the other, groaned under a load of early-shorn wool.

Speck eyed the first saloon but rode on by it. "Heard a feller say once to always pass up the first one. Shows you got willpower."

Johnny grinned. He knew this saloon had been the site of that cardsharp's *school*. "Speck, if it's all of a whatness to you, I'd rather clean up first."

Speck reined in at the square frame front of the second saloon, stepped down and wrapped his reins through a ring in the hitching post. "You wash the outside and I'll wash the inside."

They had a little money—not much. Larramore had advanced them a few dollars last fall. He owed them for a winter's work, so they would have plenty when they found him. Johnny had counted his money several times before leaving the cow camp, and now he counted it again. Main thing he wanted to begin with was a change of clothes. Those he wore had spent a hard winter, washed periodically in the river, beaten with a rock and slept on to press some of the wrinkles out.

After a while, with new-bought clothes bundled under his arm, he walked into a barbershop which advertised a bathtub. The barber was busy shaving a customer. "Have a seat, cowboy."

Johnny picked up a copy of the weekly *San Angelo Standard,* looking hopefully for items about people he knew. He didn't find his father's name in it, but he hadn't expected to. Baker Fristo was just a little rancher, and he didn't get to town much. Johnny read the trespass and cattle brand notices and shook his head in doubt over ads for patent medicines supposed to cure everything from adenoids to hemorrhoids.

Finishing the paper, he began wondering idly about the man reclining in the barber chair. He couldn't tell much except that the customer was very tall, had a new black suit, and wore a pair of high-laced shoes on feet that probably were more used to boots. A new broad-brimmed black hat and a suit coat hung on a rack by the front door.

Rancher, probably. Or a cattle buyer.

The barber was as talkative as Speck Quitman. "Folks say you've bought a ranch up on the Colorado

River, Milam." The man named Milam couldn't answer. The barber was scraping whiskers from his jaw. "Yes, sir," the barber went on, "I was up in that Colorado City country once. Sand country, it is, and good for cows. Man don't go stumblin' around over rocks all the time."

The customer had a firm, deep voice. "Any country is good, Jess, when you own a piece of it yourself."

The barber wiped soap off of his blade. "Used to think that way myself, till I lost my little place in the big panic. Found out it's easier to scrape chins than to try and scrape a livin' off a piece of hard-scrabble land. But, then, I reckon you wouldn't buy anything but a good place, Milam. Bet you and Miss Cora are goin' to be real happy."

"We will," the man said. "She'll be mighty pleased with the place, the way I've got it fixed up for her."

"When you takin' her?"

"We're leavin' tomorrow mornin', takin' the Sonora Mail to San Angelo."

The barber finished. As the customer stood up, Johnny saw that the tall man was around forty—maybe a little more. The outdoors had weathered him badly. His hair showed streaks of gray, but his moustache was still coal black. Crowtracks were etched at the corners of keen gray eyes that looked as if they had seen aplenty of hardship. For a moment those eyes lighted on Johnny. They were not unfriendly, but they looked as if they could read whatever was in a man's mind. Johnny nodded, wondering what it was about this stranger that made him feel suddenly uncomfortable.

"Howdy," said the man Milam, and that was all. He put on his hat and coat, paid the barber and left.

The barber turned to Johnny. "Shave? Haircut?"

"Both. And then a long, slow bath." Seating himself, Johnny jerked his chin toward the door. "Who was that?"

"Him? Why, friend, I thought everybody knew Milam Haggard."

"Name sounds kind of familiar."

"He was a Texas Ranger down on the Rio Grande. Married Miss Cora Hays here, and she talked him into takin' off the star. He's been off up the country, buyin' them a place to live."

Johnny stared out the open door. He vaguely remembered now. "This Haggard, he's got a name for bein' a bulldog in a fight, hasn't he?"

The barber shook his head knowingly. "A man couldn't have a better friend than Milam Haggard. Or a worse enemy. There's no end to what he'll do for a man he thinks is in the right. He's been known to ride fifty miles in the rain to fetch medicine to a sick Mexican kid. But break the law and you got trouble. He hates an outlaw. He sticks to a trail, Milam does. I don't suppose he ever let a man get away, once he ever got the scent. I recollect one time he trailed a pair of horse thieves plumb down into Mexico. I seen him come back leadin' their horses. Their gunbelts was looped around the saddlehorns, and the saddles was empty. Milam never did talk about them hunts. But he didn't have to."

With bold snips of the sharp scissors the barber took off Johnny's winter growth of hair. "Miss Cora, she made him turn in his badge and put up his guns. She was afraid someday somebody would be a-bringin' *his* saddle in empty."

Johnny took a slow soak in the barber's tub, lazily enjoying the luxury of castile soap. Out in a cow

camp, a man was lucky to have plain old lye soap that
took off the hide along with the dirt. Finished, he
tucked the bundle of dirty clothes under his arm,
mounted his horse and walked him to the saloon.
Speck's horse was still hitched out in front, head
down, one hind foot turned up in rest. Johnny shook
his head. Likely as not Speck would forget that animal and leave him standing out here all day. Johnny
untied the horse and led him to a wagonyard with his
own. Might as well turn the horses loose in the
stableman's corral and give them some feed; they
weren't going anywhere today.

Unsaddling, he asked the stableman, "All right if
we bed down over here tonight, me and my partner?
We won't bother nothin'."

Hotels were for ranchers, drummers and the like.
Cowboys generally slept in the wagonyard or down
on the riverbank.

"Help yourself. Just don't be doin' no smokin'
around that hay. I'd hate to sell you a burned-down
barn." Critically, the stableman looked Johnny over.
"You couldn't pay for it noway."

Walking back, Johnny told himself it was fortu-
nate Speck didn't have enough money on him to get
into a poker game. Put Speck to work in the country
and he was usually worth his wages. But turn him
loose in town and he was likely to kick over the
traces, bedazzled by the flash of cards and the slosh
of whisky. It was like he hadn't grown up, and maybe
never would.

Johnny had let Speck have three dollars this
morning. He figured that wasn't enough to get him
drunk or into a poker game. Entering the saloon, he
found out how wrong he was. Speck pushed away

from a gaming table and threw his hands up in a gesture of defeat. "That cleans me." He spotted Johnny. "Hey, partner, come here and give me enough for a fresh start. I'm just about to clean these fellers' plow."

Johnny covered his impatience with a grin he didn't mean. "Looks to me like it's *your* plow that shines."

"Aw, Johnny . . ." But Speck could see Johnny meant to be firm. He didn't beg. He leaned on Johnny, looking instinctively to his partner to help him keep his nose clean.

One of the gamblers called to the bartender, "Lige, give them cowboys a drink. I'm payin' for it with their own money."

Speck and Johnny leaned work-flattened bellies against the short granite-topped bar. Speck lifted his glass and said, "Here's to Larramore and his speedy arrival."

Johnny almost choked. He knew he had tasted worse whisky, but he couldn't remember just when. Speck had a fondness for the stuff; Johnny could take it or leave it alone. This kind was better left alone.

A man appeared in the saloon's open door. He started to walk in, then stopped abruptly, seeing Johnny and Speck. Quickly he backed out and walked off up the street.

Johnny straightened. "Speck, that was Larramore."

Speck hadn't noticed. "Maybe he didn't see us."

"He saw us. He backed out like somebody had shot at him. I don't like the smell of it."

Speck frowned. "You don't think he would . . ." He broke off, doubt in his eyes. "You know, he just might."

Johnny nodded grimly. "Let's go find out."

Larramore was walking briskly away. Johnny

called, but the cow trader appeared not to hear. Johnny and Speck broke into a long trot and caught up with him in front of a general store.

"Mister Larramore," Johnny said, coming up behind him, "just a minute."

Larramore turned and looked surprised. "By George, it's Speck and Johnny. Wasn't expectin' you-all till Friday."

Johnny said, "Old Man Hoskins told us to come on in. So we're here, Mister Larramore, and we sure do need our money."

Larramore's face was blank. He was watching someone walking up the street. "Money? What money?"

Johnny's voice hardened. "We put in six months of work for you, Larramore." He wasn't using the *mister* now. "You promised us twenty dollars a month. Now we want to get paid."

Johnny was hardly aware of footsteps on the plank walk behind him, or of a man with a badge who passed them and started into the general store. But Larramore had seen him, and he raised his voice.

"I've already paid you. I paid both of you at the ranch. What do you mean now, tryin' to browbeat me into payin' you again?"

The man in the doorway stopped and turned, his attention caught.

Speck Quitman's face boiled full of rage. He grabbed both fists full of Larramore's shirt. "You're a liar! All you ever gave us was a few dollars advance last fall. Now, damn you, pay up!"

Watching the sheriff, Larramore stood his ground. "Get your hands off of me, you halfwit! I won't stand for bein' robbed!"

The insult to Speck made Johnny clench his fists. "*You're* the one who's a thief, Larramore."

The sheriff had heard enough. He stepped up and placed a big hand firmly over Speck's fist, his eyes stern. "Turn him loose, cowboy."

Speck turned angrily upon the intruder, but his mouth shut as he saw the badge.

A cow trader has to be quick on his feet or he doesn't survive. Larramore was quick. "Sheriff, it's a good thing you came by. These boys are tryin' to pull a fast shuffle on me."

The sheriff's grim eyes flashed from one man to the other. "All right, everybody simmer down a little. Tell me what the trouble is."

Larramore spoke quickly, heading off Speck and Johnny. "I hired these two last fall to watch over some cattle I was winterin' down on the Devil's River. The other day I picked up the cattle and paid these men. Now they're tryin' to claim they've still got wages comin'. It's not my fault if they've drunk it up or lost it playin' poker."

Johnny said, "He's a liar, sheriff."

The sheriff frowned. He leaned close and sniffed suspiciously. "You-all *have* been drinkin'. I can smell it."

Johnny said, "Just one is all I've had. It was bought for me. We're not lyin' to you, sheriff. *He* is."

The sheriff studied Speck. "Seems to me I remember you boys. You was in town last fall." His eyes lighted. "Sure, you lost your wad down yonder tryin' to beat one of them Angelo gamblers. You was dead broke."

Larramore cut in, "That's right, sheriff. I gave them a job. Do a man a favor and he'll spit on you every time."

Johnny protested, "He *hasn't* paid us."

The sheriff looked at Johnny's new clothes. "If you haven't been paid, where did those duds come from?"

Johnny could tell the sheriff was almost convinced now, and not in their favor. He started to tell about the advance Larramore had given them last fall, but he realized it would sound hollow. How many cowboys could keep anything all winter out of a fall advance?

Johnny had a sudden thought. "Old Man Hoskins knows. Why don't you ask him?"

A shade of doubt appeared in the sheriff's eyes. "Ely Hoskins? Sure, his word is as good as his bond. But it's a long ways out there."

"If you're interested in the truth, you'll go ask him."

Larramore said, "They're just stallin', sheriff. They're caught in a lie. They belong in jail."

Speck Quitman exploded. His fist came up and caught Larramore full in the face. Larramore staggered backward against the clapboard wall of the general store. For a second Johnny thought the trader was going to fall through the front window. Speck roared forward to follow up his punch, but the sheriff reached out and grabbed him by the collar. With a sudden thrust of his mighty arm, the lawman threw Speck off balance and sent him sprawling backward into the dust of the street.

"That done it!" the sheriff thundered. "I was halfway inclined to go along with you boys, but now I'm goin' to let you sweat awhile in the jailhouse."

Larramore swayed, one hand behind him to brace him away from the wall, the other lifted to his face. His nose was bleeding.

Johnny urged, "Sheriff, Speck's hotheaded, and

what he did wasn't smart. But it don't change the fact
that Larramore's lyin'. Give us a chance. Go talk to
Old Man Hoskins."

The sheriff scowled down at Speck Quitman, who
was shakily pushing himself up out of the dust. The
lawman pondered. Something about Larramore
seemed to make him uncertain. "I don't know what
I'm wastin' my time for, but I'll do it. I'll send a man
out to talk to old Ely. Till then, you boys are goin' to
enjoy Sutton County's hospitality. Behind bars!" He
glanced at Larramore. "I'm expectin' you to stay in
town till I get the straight of this."

Larramore nodded, holding his handkerchief to his
face. "Sure, sheriff, anything you say." He avoided
looking at the cowboys.

The sheriff took hold of Johnny's and Speck's
arms. "Come on." They walked up the street, the sheriff holding them tightly. The few people who were outdoors paused to look. It was evident the two were
under arrest.

A tall man and a woman stepped out of a store and
almost directly into their path. The man caught the
woman's arm and moved her gently aside. Johnny
recognized Milam Haggard. The handsome young
woman would be the wife the barber had been telling
about. Her eyes touched Johnny's, and he thought he
saw sympathy there.

But he found no sympathy in Milam Haggard. The
longtime Ranger stared with stern gray eyes. Any
friendliness he might have shown in the barbershop
was gone now. It wouldn't matter to Haggard what
the trouble was about. He could tell the cowboys
were in custody. That was enough for him to pass his
judgment.

The sheriff took his hand from Johnny's arm long enough to tip his hat. "Howdy, Cora . . . Milam."

The three walked by. Johnny glanced back, for no particular reason. Milam Haggard was still watching him.

II

A bugle sounded. Johnny Fristo awoke to the rattle of trace chains and the clatter of horses' hoofs. The Sonora Mail was leaving for San Angelo.

Johnny opened his eyes and glanced up at the barred window. Sunrise. He arose stiffly from the hard cot and stretched his back to try to work the ache out of it. The air was cool and fresh. Johnny's movement aroused Speck Quitman, who peered dourly at him a moment, then swung his sock feet down to the floor and started probing around sleepy-eyed, trying to find his boots.

A limping man entered the jail's front door, carrying a covered platter. "You boys up?" the pleasant old jailer asked needlessly. "Brought you-all some breakfast."

He unlocked the cell door and dragged in a small table. He did it carelessly, as if not even considering that the two prisoners could easily jump him and get away. He had brought a big mess of scrambled eggs with pieces of fried beef alongside, and some biscuits. "Hope you fellers don't mind eatin' off of the platter. Too far to pack extra dishes."

Leaving the cell door wide open, he went to the stove and picked up the coffee pot. "Now, don't you boys go gettin' the wrong idea; we don't treat all our prisoners this good. But I figure you-all been out in a cow camp all winter and ain't had no eggs. Besides, like I was tellin' the sheriff, it's probably that Larramore who ought to be in here 'stead of you two."

Johnny and Speck went after the eggs like a pair of starved wolves. The talkative jailer sipped the scalding black coffee, his lips immune to the burn. "I used to cowboy, too, till I got stove up. I looked you two over and decided you was all right. Besides, I heard about some cow deals Larramore was mixed up in. He's no deacon in the church."

Johnny asked, "Hear anything yet from Old Man Hoskins?"

"Nope. Thought he might be in the crowd that was down while ago to see Milam and Cora Haggard off on the Sonora Mail. But he wasn't." He smiled, remembering. "My, she sure did look handsome. Folks was afraid she would wait around and be an old maid, but I guess she was just waitin' for the right man. And she got him." He paused. "You know about Milam Haggard?"

Johnny nodded. "Some."

"*Mucho hombre,* that Milam. Sure did hate to see him turn in his badge. But I expect most of the devilment is over anyway. Country's turned respectable. Milam has outlived his time as a lawman. We don't need his kind of lawin' anymore. This is the '90s now, and we're about as modern as we can ever get."

Eventually the sheriff came, his face creasing as he saw the open cell door. "Ad," he spoke sharply to the jailer, "this is a jailhouse, not a *hotel*. One of these days somebody's goin' to walk right out over you."

Standing up, the jailer said defensively, "I wouldn't do it for just anybody, but these boys are all right. Like I was tellin' you last night . . ."

The sheriff nodded, his rueful gaze passing from Johnny to Speck and back again. "I remember what you told me, and it turns out you were right. Boys, you can go."

Johnny smiled. "So you heard from Old Man Hoskins?"

The sheriff was chagrined. "Didn't have to. I just found out Larramore sneaked off to the edge of town awhile ago and caught the stage hack for San Angelo. If he'd been on the square, he'd have stayed here like I told him."

Johnny swore. "Damn him! He's tryin' to get off and keep from payin' us what we got comin'."

The sheriff shook his head. "He'll pay. If you boys will get saddled up and put them ponies through their paces, you can get to Angelo ahead of the hack. Go see the sheriff there. I'll write you a letter to give him. He'll see that Larramore pays what he owes you or he'll shove him way back in jail and forget where the key is at."

Speck and Johnny waited impatiently while the lawman scribbled a note. The officer said, "I'd go myself, only I just got word of some trouble down in the south end of the county that's liable to lead to a shootin' if I don't stop it."

Speck said with bitterness, "How am I goin' to explain to my Aunt Pru about me spendin' the night in jail? And all for nothin'."

The old jailer grinned. "Well, look at the bright side: you had supper, breakfast, and a bed, and it didn't cost you a cent."

"Some bed," gritted Speck. "I've slept on rocks that was softer."

The jailer grinned again. "We don't advertise for repeat business."

Johnny folded the letter the sheriff had given him and stuck it in his pocket. "One thing sure, *we* don't intend to come back."

The sheriff followed them down to the wagonyard and watched while they saddled their horses. "Stop in at Pete Smith's ranch halfway to Angelo and tell him

I said lend you a pair of fresh horses. And one more thing: don't try to do nothin' on your own. Just go around that hack and get to Angelo ahead of it. Let the Tom Green County sheriff take care of Larramore his own way. That's his job. You-all leave Larramore alone."

Anger edged Johnny's voice. "He owes us more than wages now, sheriff. He owes us for a night in jail."

The sheriff repeated, "Don't you-all do anything, do you hear me?"

Johnny and Speck heard, but they made no reply. They rode out of the wagonyard gate, touched spurs to their horses and moved into an easy lope on the mail and freight road that led north toward San Angelo.

Twisting along at the foot of the hills, the trail made a slow climb toward the top of the divide which separated the sprawling watershed of the Devil's River from that of the three Conchos. From where the cowboys rode, rainwater would drain generally southward, first to countless draws and creeks, then to the Devil's River and finally by a tortuous, canyon-cutting route to the Rio Grande.

Spring had come with color and hope to this high, rocky limestone country known as the Edwards Plateau. Winter rains had preserved the holdover moisture stored last fall, and now fresh grass rose tender and green amid the tall brown leavings of last year's bluestem growth. Cattle already were slicking off, shedding their coarse winter hair. Frisky calves were fat and shiny.

Johnny and Speck came upon a band of sheep, scattered to graze on an open flat where the grass was shorter and more to their liking. Fat young lambs lifted their heads to watch the riders passing. Many of them scampered away bleating. A Mexican herder stood up at the cowboys' approach and nodded a silent greeting, his eyes narrowed in distrust. Too often the *gringo* did not come in peace.

Johnny asked, "How long since the mail hack passed this way?"

The herder just stared at him, as if he did not understand. Speck broke in to repeat the question in a halting, broken Spanish. The herder did not smile at Speck's mistakes. But neither did he give a clear answer. "*¿Quién sabe?* A while. I have no watch, *señor*."

Speck seemed disposed to try again, this time in anger, but Johnny said, "Let it go, Speck. That's all the answer we'll get. We're makin' some gain, and we'll catch up."

They moved on, putting the horses into an easy lope and holding them in it as long as they dared. Every so often Johnny would pull down to a trot. Usually he would have to call to Speck, who didn't stop until he saw that Johnny was going to, with or without him.

"Speck, we can't make it if we ride these horses down."

They would trot along a mile or so, then Speck would impatiently spur into a lope again. Johnny noticed Speck wasn't doing any talking. That in itself was a bad sign. The rusty-haired cowboy's jaw took a hard, angry set, and his eyes were narrowed.

Speck was talking inside, to himself. Johnny knew the signs. When Speck was like this the inner heat would crackle and build until there had to be an explosion of some kind. There was no other outlet. That

was a side of Speck Quitman most people didn't
know about, for it didn't often show. Most regarded
him as a scatter-brained cowboy with a lot of bark
and no bite. But Johnny had seen him bite a few
times. He didn't like it.

They came out atop the divide in a wind-rippled
sea of short green grass. Speck reined up and stood
in his stirrups, peering out through a scattering of
liveoak trees which were shedding their old leaves
and putting on a new set.

"Johnny, I think I see the hack up yonder, ahead
of us."

Johnny squinted. It took him a minute, but finally
he saw it too. Speck turned in his saddle and untied
his warbag. He dug around in it, then pulled out a six-
shooter, wrapped in oilskin. It was old and tarnished,
and on one side a knife-whittled piece of mesquite
wood had replaced the original black rubber grip.
Relic though it was, Speck prized it above anything
else he owned. He had bought it from a broke cow-
puncher when he was only fifteen, and he had carried
it around with him ever since. He had given it the
loving care a man might give a horse. He had never
used it in anger, though sometimes Johnny Fristo got
a cold, ominous feeling that Speck hoped someday
he could. Speck began to punch cartridges into it.

Tightly Johnny said, "Speck, you got no use for
that thing. The sheriff told us to go to the law in Angelo, not to try handlin' Larramore ourselves."

"It wasn't the sheriff he cheated. It wasn't the
sheriff that had to spend the night in the Sonora jail
like some drunk sheepherder."

"Speck, you better put that thing back into your
warbag before you do somethin' you'll wish you
hadn't. What if you was to accidentally shoot him? A

dead man don't pay no wages." He thought at first Speck might be listening to him. But Speck shoved the loaded pistol into his waistband.

"I'm not fixin' to shoot him. But I sure do intend to scare him to death."

Speck's spurs tinkled as he touched them to his horse and surged forward. Johnny held back a moment, trying to figure some way to reason with him. Then he hurried to catch up. "Speck, listen to me. The sheriff made sense. This is the kind of thing they got sheriffs *for*."

"A man ought to stomp his own snakes. And Larramore is a snake."

"We can make a little *vuelta* around them and get to Angelo first. Larramore won't have any idea we're around. We can spring the sheriff on him as a surprise."

But Speck was hot as a wolf, and he was riding, not listening. The thought of that pistol made a cold chill run down Johnny's back. Somehow it always had. He would as soon touch a rattlesnake.

Still, he knew the only way he could stop Speck now would be with a club. All Johnny could do was stay close and try to keep things from getting too badly out of hand. They were partners, right or wrong, smart or otherwise. Several times before, Johnny had come close to riding off in disgust and leaving Speck. But always in the end he would shrug and stay with him.

He stayed with him now.

Ahead of them the trail took a bend around a big motte of liveoak trees to avoid a wheel-breaking gully. Speck cut across, Johnny close behind him. They loped around the heavy motte and came back into the trail ahead of the stage hack. Speck slid his horse to a stop. He raised the pistol to signal the driver to halt.

It would have been hard to gauge which showed strongest in the driver's face—anger or alarm. A robbery on the Sonora Mail was unheard of! "What do you two peckerwoods want?" he demanded. "We got nothin' on board here that's worth stealin'."

Speck Quitman replied in a tense voice that didn't sound at all like his. "Don't fret yourself, mister. We didn't stop you to steal anything."

"Then put that cannon away before you scare the lady!"

Johnny pulled his horse up beside Speck's. "For God's sake, Speck, put that damned old smoke-belcher down. We're fixin' to get ourselves in a mess of trouble."

Under the rolled-up side canvas he could see the frightened face of Cora Haggard, her hands tightly clutching Milam Haggard's arm. Haggard stared at the cowboys, his gray eyes challenging and unafraid. But he was helpless, for he wore no gun. In the seat behind the Haggards, the trader Larramore was trying to crouch down out of sight.

The hack driver had a heavy brown moustache and a loud, harsh voice. "If you didn't come to steal nothin', put that gun back where it belongs. Somebody might get hurt. Besides, you're stoppin' the U.S. mail. That could get you sent to the pen."

Johnny decided it was time for him to do the talking. Speck wasn't getting them anywhere but in trouble. "Mister, we don't mean to hurt anybody, and we're sure not fixin' to tamper with the mail. But you got a passenger who left Sonora owin' us money, and we want it."

"Cowboy," said the driver, "your private feuds ain't any concern of the Sonora Mail. The man is a passenger. You take up your complaints with the law."

Speck Quitman waved the pistol. "We brought our own law. Larramore, you get yourself down from there, and be right spry about it!"

Larramore stood up partway, his head touching the canvas. "They're lyin'. They come to rob me!"

Milam Haggard spoke in a rock-steady voice: "You heard what the driver said, boys. I don't know anything about the merit of your claim on this man, but I do know that the way you're doin' this constitutes robbery in the eyes of the law. I suggest you stand back and let this hack go on."

"Mister Haggard," Johnny said, "there's already *been* a robbery, and it was us that got robbed."

Haggard studied him a moment with eyes so stern that Johnny couldn't hold his gaze against them. "I remember you. The Sonora sheriff had you in tow yesterday. That doesn't make your argument sound very good to me."

Johnny reached for his shirt pocket. "I've got a letter here . . ."

Impatience jabbed its spurs into Speck Quitman. "Forget the letter. We're takin' Larramore off this stage and gettin' our money!"

Angrily Haggard said, "There's a woman in this hack. You put that gun away!"

Haggard's severe voice got through to Speck where Johnny's pleading hadn't. Speck was a little afraid of the man. He lowered the barrel, but he rode around closer to Larramore. "How about it, Larramore? You gettin' down, or do I have to shoot you in the leg or somethin'?"

Face white, Larramore began climbing out. "All right, I'm comin'." Stepping to the ground, he turned to plead with Haggard and the driver. "Are you goin' to let them get away with this?"

The driver said, "Mister, I got no gun. Neither has Milam."

Johnny held his breath. Now he began to feel the thing was going to go over all right. Maybe there wasn't going to be any more trouble. He rode around to the off side of the hack, where Larramore stood. He dismounted a couple of paces from the cow trader. Speck's anger gave way to anticipation, and he stepped down from the saddle.

"All right, Larramore, a hundred dollars apiece."

Larramore replied shakily, "I got the money in my bag." He turned and lifted a canvas grip out of the hack. Speck shoved the pistol into his waistband and eagerly stepped closer to look as Larramore opened the bag. The trader reached inside. "There now, I've got it."

He brought his hand out with a short-barreled Colt revolver.

Johnny didn't hesitate. He jumped at the trader. Larramore squeezed the trigger. The hammer fell on the empty shell he kept in the cylinder for safety, the empty shell he had forgotten in his anxiety. But the next cartridge would be a live one. Johnny grabbed the man's wrist. They struggled.

The woman screamed. Haggard started putting her off the hack on the other side to get her away from the fight. At the same time he was shouting, "You fools, be careful with that pistol! You'll kill somebody!"

The team caught the excitement and danced nervously, ready to run. Badly as he might have wanted to jump, the driver couldn't afford to. He had all he could handle, holding the team.

Larramore brought up his knee and struck Johnny a hard blow to the stomach. Johnny bent a little and let go. Larramore stepped clear and leveled the pistol. As he squeezed the trigger, Speck Quitman caught him from behind and spoiled his aim.

The flash blinded Johnny for an instant. The explosion set his ears to ringing. But he heard a faint cry from the woman on the other side.

The team ran. The driver jammed one foot against the brake and sawed hard at the lines to prevent them from getting completely away. As the hack pulled forward, Johnny saw horror in Larramore's eyes. Larramore pitched the gun away. Johnny spun on his heel.

Cora Haggard was going down. Milam Haggard grabbed her and cried out, "Cora!" Gently he eased her to the grass.

The three men who had been fighting stood stiff and silent now, stunned. They saw the spread of crimson across the woman's white blouse. The color had drained from her face. Her hand reached up and clutched at Haggard's shirt. She gasped, "Milam, I love you." Then the hand dropped away.

Milam Haggard cried again, "Cora!" He pulled her against him as if to try to hold her away from death. But death came despite him, and she lay lifeless in his arms.

Larramore's wits came back to him. He pointed at Johnny and shouted, "That one did it, Haggard! He's the one who fired the gun."

The lie caught Johnny by surprise, and for a moment he could not speak. He stood with mouth open and dry. He tried for words that wouldn't come. A horrified thought ran through his mind:

Haggard will believe him.

Somehow he managed to stammer, "No . . . no . . . I didn't! *He* had the gun! He was shootin' at *me!*"

But he was too late. Larramore had seized the advantage. He had said it first, and Haggard believed him. Johnny could see it in the violent hatred that welled into the tall man's eyes.

The hack driver fought the team under control and circled back. He jumped to the ground and stared wide-eyed at Milam Haggard, who still knelt, holding his wife. The driver breathed in horror, "Milam, for God's sake . . ."

Johnny cried, "Driver, he thinks it was me that killed her. It was Larramore. Tell him. You saw it."

The driver turned slowly, his face ashen. "I saw nothin'. I was too busy tryin' to hold that team. But you boys held us up, and you was robbin' a passenger. That speaks for itself."

Milam Haggard buried his face against his wife's slender neck. He held her, his shoulders trembling, while the other four men stood in helpless silence. At last the driver took a slow step forward. "Milam, we best put her aboard and take her back to Sonora."

Milam Haggard raised his head. Gently he lowered his wife to the ground. His gaze fell upon the pistol Larramore had tossed away. Johnny saw the intention in his eyes, and he stepped forward quickly. He grabbed up the gun just as Haggard was about to leap for it.

Desperate, Johnny said, "Mister Haggard, Larramore lied to you. I didn't shoot her."

Tears swam in Haggard's eyes, but a cold fury showed through. His slow-measured words were edged with steel. "I'll remember you."

"Please, Mister Haggard, listen to me . . ."

"I'll take my wife home and bury her amongst her people. Then I'll come lookin' for you. You can stay here, or you can run, it makes me no difference.

Whether it takes me a week or a year, whether I ride twenty miles or a thousand, I'll find you two. And when I find you, *I'll kill you!*"

"Mister Haggard . . ." Johnny broke off, for Haggard had turned his back. He had shut his ears and his mind.

Gently the driver and Larramore lifted the woman's body. Haggard climbed into the hack and took her into his arms. The driver turned to Johnny and Speck. "Was I you boys, I'd go back to Sonora and throw myself on the mercy of the court. Maybe the court will have some. There'll be no mercy in Milam Haggard!"

He climbed up, took the reins, turned the hack around and started back down the trail toward Sonora.

Johnny and Speck watched until the hack was gone out of sight. Speck finally broke the silence, and he was crying. "It was my fault, Johnny. I ought to've listened to you." Tears rolled down his freckled cheeks. Fear was taking a grip on him. Speck could shift from one emotion to another like he could change shirts. "We got to go some place, Johnny, and we got to go quick. Let's head for Mexico. It's only a hundred miles to the Rio Grande."

Johnny's voice was tight with shock. "And what do we do when we get there? We got no friends down there, and we got no money. We don't even speak the language enough to get by."

"But it's Mexico. The law couldn't touch us down there."

"It's not the law we got to worry about most, it's Milam Haggard. That river wouldn't even slow him down. He'd just keep a-huntin' us, and we'd just keep a-runnin'. And wherever we went, we'd be *gringos*. We'd stand out like the Twin Mountains."

Speck's eyes were swimming in tears. "But what can we do? If we stay here he'll kill us."

"Texas is a mighty big country. He can't search it all. There are places west of here where you could drop a whole army and never find it. Maybe in time he'll get tired of lookin'."

Speck said weakly, "I bet he don't ever quit. He looks like the kind that'll stay on a trail till the day he dies."

Johnny's jaw set firmly. That was the way Haggard had looked to him, too. But a man couldn't just sit and wait for somebody to come and kill him.

Speck said, "We got to get us a little money, Johnny. We could borrow somethin' from my Aunt Pru in San Angelo."

Johnny nodded soberly. "We better get ridin'."

It occurred to him then that he still held Larramore's pistol. He stared at it in loathing. He drew back his arm and hurled the pistol as hard as he could, into a liveoak motte.

He swung onto his horse and headed north toward San Angelo.

III

They rode in by night, following the stage road that crossed the South Concho at the flood-ruined settlement of Ben Ficklin. Three miles farther on, they rode by the stone buildings of old Fort Concho, abandoned a few years ago by the army when the Indian problems were over. Civilians lived there now. Most of the buildings were dark, for working people had gone to bed.

But across the North Concho, lamps still glowed along Chadbourne and Oakes and Concho Avenue. Horses stood in headsdown, hipshot patience at hitchracks in front of the Nimitz Hotel, the Legal Tender and the other saloons. Johnny and Speck rested their horses at the steep south bank of the quiet-moving river and waited in darkness, watching. Nearby stood the Oakes Street Bridge, but they had purposely shied away from it, just as they had shied away from all travelers on the road today.

Speck said, "I hear a horse comin' across. That wooden plankin' sure does make a noise at night."

Johnny nodded. "We best skip the bridge anyhow. It'd land us smack on Concho Avenue amongst all the saloons."

"There's a shallow crossin' a little ways upriver. We could use that and not run into anybody."

They moved past the deep section known as Dead Man's Hole to the shallow water. They walked the horses across quietly, trying not to splash. But their stealth was thwarted when a couple of stray dogs picked them up.

"Git!" Johnny hissed, wishing he had something to throw at the barking dogs. "Git, I say!"

Anxiously he looked around him in the darkness, afraid someone would come. A man in a picket shack stuck his head out the door and yelled angrily at the dogs to shut up. He didn't appear to see Speck and Johnny.

The huge Tom Green County courthouse, with its high stone walls and its tall cupola, loomed massively in the dim moonlight. It stood back well away from the river, with most of the town lying east and south of it. Some new development was building up in the courthouse area. Johnny had heard someone say San Angelo's population was around five thousand now, but he doubted it. It wouldn't be that big in a hundred years. San Angelo was a ranch town. With the army gone, it was dependent upon cattle and sheep, upon small farms scattered along the three Concho Rivers, and upon the freighting of supplies to ranches and settlements which lay west and south all the way to the Pecos and the Rio Grande.

Johnny had always enjoyed coming here, for San Angelo was the biggest town he had ever seen. Seemed like there was always something to watch, from a backlot badger fight up to horse races and steer roping. Holiday-seeking cowboys rode in from a hundred miles away, for this was a tolerant town that understood a man's letting off steam after months of isolation on a ranch. Long as he didn't hurt anybody and paid for what he broke, no one bothered him much.

They gave him his money's worth and showed him a time.

Since the shooting, Johnny and Speck hadn't done any talking. They had ridden in silence, each nursing his thoughts, sick with remorse and dread. Johnny didn't know how many times he had seen that woman's blood-drained face before his eyes, how many times he had heard her gasp and had seen her die in Milam Haggard's arms.

Now, in the familiar streets of San Angelo, some of the somber mood lifted. But not all of it.

Speck said sorrowfully, "It sure does hurt to come a-sneakin' in this away, like a pair of cur dogs followin' all the back alleys. I always liked to ride in on Concho Avenue screechin' like a wild Indian and lettin' the whole town know I was somebody come."

Johnny knew the ache that throbbed in Speck now, for Speck had grown up here, had played barefoot in these dirt streets when this was little more than a hide-hunter camp and a whisky village for Negro soldiers and white officers in the fort across the river.

Speck's voice was melancholy. "I sure hate havin' to leave here. It was hard, livin' with Aunt Pru, but I always did love this town. I fished up and down these rivers. I knew every horse and burro and dog by its name. I bet I could still show you the big old pecan tree where I climbed up out of the water the time of the Ben Ficklin flood." He shook his head. "A queen of a town, she is . . . a cowboy's town."

Johnny said, "Maybe things'll work out someday."

Speck's voice broke. "You saw Haggard's eyes. We can't *never* come back!"

They held up once and pulled back into an alley as a surrey passed with a man and a woman riding in it. Johnny caught the high lift of the woman's laughter and knew she would be one of the "girls" from down on West Concho, by the river. Bitterness touched him as he thought how off-center fate could be, a lady like Cora Haggard lying cold and still in death, while a woman of this kind went right on living, squealing in empty-headed merriment. Why couldn't it have been this one who had died? On reflection, he knew the thought was childish. One person could not take another's place when it came time to die. This woman had no responsibility toward Cora Haggard. That responsibility lay with Larramore and Speck and himself.

Aunt Pru lived alone in a small frame house back from Chadbourne Street. The house was dark as Johnny and Speck rode up to the rear of it. They tied their horses to the picket fence.

Speck said, "Careful now, and don't trip over a faucet. That new waterworks has piped water right to everybody's back step. Next thing you know they'll be wantin' it in the house." He moved up to the small back porch and knocked. Johnny heard no sign of life. Speck knocked again and called softly, "Aunt Pru!"

In a moment a pair of feet scuffed across the wooden floor. A glow went up as a lamp was lighted. Aunt Pru opened the door cautiously and extended the lamp in front of her to light the young men's faces while she held the door ready for a quick closing. She had pulled a cotton housecoat on over her nightgown. Her hair was rolled up. Sleepy-eyed, she squinted. She said with a start, "Speck!"

Anxiously Speck said, "Aunt Pru, would you please get the light out of our faces and let us come in the house? We got to talk to you."

The graying woman stared suspiciously as she lowered the lamp and opened the door wider. "Very well, come on in." When they were inside she said sharply, "Speck, let me smell your breath." He leaned close. She sniffed. Her eyes showed disbelief. "You don't appear to've been drinking. What on earth are you doing out at this time of night? Decent folk are all in bed."

Speck avoided his aunt's eyes. He glanced at Johnny

as if seeking support. But Johnny intended to let Speck do the talking, as he usually did. Johnny had always stood in awe of this thin-faced, sharp-tongued woman.

Her gaze snapped from one to the other. "Well, there's something the matter. Speak up!"

Speck was hesitant. "Aunt Pru, there's been a little trouble."

"Trouble?" Her eyes widened. She glanced with sharp disapproval at Johnny, then back to her nephew. "I knew it; I always knew it. I knew someday you'd run too long with the wrong crowd and come dragging trouble to my door. What have you done?"

Speck's voice quavered. "Aunt Pru, we didn't go to do nothin'. It wasn't our fault, really, but we been blamed for it."

"Speck, you're evading me. What have you done?"

Speck was close to crying. "It was an accident. A woman got killed this mornin'. Man who done it, he hollered right quick that it was us, and they believed him. We're on the run, Aunt Pru. We got to run or die."

The tall, thin woman stared in horror, her hands coming up to her cheeks, her mouth open. "A killing! You've gotten mixed up in a killing!"

"It wasn't our fault. We just got the blame for it, is all."

She didn't seem to hear. She turned away from him, crying aloud, raising her face to look up at the ceiling, then dropping her chin.

"Aunt Pru, we hoped maybe you could lend us a little money. We'll send it back to you soon's we can. We wouldn't ask it of you, only we got cheated out of a whole winter's pay. That's what caused the trouble in the first place."

She turned on him with an unexpected savageness.

"Money! You bring disgrace to this house, to our name, and then you have the gall to come and beg me for money?"

Speck took a step backward, astonished at her reaction. "We wouldn't ask you, Aunt Pru, but we're desperate. We'll pay you back, I promise."

"Promise! How many times have you made me promises, Speck, and how few times have you lived up to them? Promised you'd go to school? Promised you wouldn't run around with riffraff?" Her furious eyes cut to Johnny. "You promised you'd look for respectable work, but you joined a group of common cowboys and drank whisky and caroused and made a sinner of yourself. You've drunk and gambled and debauched yourself with those painted women down on Concho and left me in shame."

Speck dropped his chin and stood in red-faced silence while she railed at him: "I knew this would happen someday. You were born with the mark of sin on you, and now it's the brand of Cain. When my sister came to me to have her baby, and no ring on her finger, I knew the mark was on you and you would come to a bad end. But I tried, God knows how I tried. I raised you and kept you because you were my sister's baby. I gave you a home and fed you and tried to teach you righteousness. But all the time I knew someday the stain of sin would show. I knew you were born to hang."

Speck's shoulders slumped. Tears rolled down his cheeks. He looked like a dog driven into a corner and whipped, a dog that had no wish to fight back.

"All these years," she drove on relentlessly, "I've known this day would come. I could have thrown her out and been spared this shame. But I was a Christian woman."

Johnny listened with anger swelling in him. He caught Speck's arm. "Come on, Speck, let's get out of here."

Speck edged toward the door. Aunt Pru shrilled, "That's right, run! Get on your horse and run, but you can't escape your sin. It's been on you since the day you were born!"

Johnny pushed through the door, pulling hard on Speck's arm. In the doorway Speck paused. Head still down, he didn't look up into his aunt's face. But he said brokenly, "Aunt Pru, I'm sorry."

The gaunt woman cried, "Go on, get out of here! There's been enough shame on this house already." She raised her face to the ceiling. "Oh, God, what have I done? Why do you torment me so?"

"Aunt Pru . . ."

"I've done my Christian duty. Now I'm through. Go on, and may God have mercy on you!"

Speck trembled like a child lost. Johnny let go his friend's arm and took an angry step toward the woman. But he caught himself before he loosed the torrent of fury that strained within him. He said only: "My mother was a *real* Christian woman. She'd have cut out her tongue before she would've said the things you did."

He wheeled, caught Speck's arm again and hurried him out the back gate. They swung into their saddles. Johnny said tightly, "Speck, we'll go out and see my dad. Maybe he can help us."

Speck made no effort to talk. They headed north, leaving San Angelo behind them.

For a long time they rode in silence, bone-weary and sensing the weariness of the horses. Johnny watched the reflection of the moon in the river. Speck slumped in the saddle, his head down, the torment so heavy on him that Johnny could feel the weight of it himself. At length Speck asked, "What you thinkin' about, Johnny?"

Johnny hesitated. "I guess I was thinkin' about that woman, that poor Mrs. Haggard."

"I was afraid maybe you was thinkin' about Aunt Pru."

Johnny shook his head. "I'd forgot about her," he lied.

"I wish you hadn't heard all the things she said. She's probably sorry now."

Johnny's face twisted. *She's not sorry for anybody but herself.* It occurred to him she hadn't asked a single question about Mrs. Haggard—not her name, not even how the accident had come to happen. *She's never felt sorry for anybody in her life, nobody but herself.*

"Aunt Pru's really a good woman," Speck insisted. "You just got to know her, is all. I reckon I've given her a lot of grief."

And she's enjoyed it all, Johnny thought. He had known people who seemed to thrive on misery, who seemed to enjoy feeling sorry for themselves and couldn't be happy unless they were unhappy. It never had made sense to Johnny. But he could recognize the symptoms.

Aunt Pru had them all.

Speck worried, "I just wish she hadn't said what she did in front of you, that about my mother and all." He didn't look at Johnny. "I never did want you to know. I hope you don't think none the less of me, now that you know what I am."

"It doesn't make a particle of difference."

Speck brooded. "Seems like I've known about it as long as I can remember. Aunt Pru, she told me a hundred times how she took in my mother and helped her 'hide her sin.' Then I was born, and my mother died. 'God's mercy,' Aunt Pru always said. She just kept me. Sure, she rode me pretty hard, always houndin' me about this and that and the other thing, warnin' me three times a day about hellfire. But she fed me and kept me in clothes. Always said she didn't want folks sayin' she didn't do the Christian thing by her sister's boy.

"You've seen her with her bad side showin', Johnny. But she's all the folks I got. You've had a family. Me, I just got Aunt Pru. Blood kin means a right smart to you when you have so little of it. She's my aunt, and I reckon I love her."

"Never was any question about that."

"And she loves me; I know she does."

Johnny nodded. "Sure she does, Speck." But he had his doubts.

The horses had put in a long trip, all the way from Sonora. Johnny could feel his mount about to cave in beneath him. A man could drive himself to extremes when he had a reason, but he had to consider his horse.

Sometime around midnight they halted on a sloping river bottom, where ageless native pecan trees stood like silent giants, spreading a huge canopy of fresh green leaves which blacked out all the moonlight. For countless generations the Indians had come to the three Conchos each fall to gather nuts for winter food. Now the faces had changed, but the routine had not. Come fall, people from San Angelo and all around would tramp up and down these riverbanks gathering pecans to eat or to sell.

The two staked their horses. Speck voiced concern. "We oughtn't to be stoppin'. No tellin' who's behind us, or how far."

But there was no choice, not unless a man wanted to walk off and leave a dead horse. They spread their single blankets upon the mat of fallen leaves and stretched out. Johnny was so weary he ached all over. He thought he would drop right off to sleep. But he found himself lying awake, looking up into the heavy foliage, which rustled gently in a cool early-morning breeze. The tensions of the past hours did not leave him as he had hoped they would. Lying there, it was almost as if he were still in the saddle, still plodding those endless miles, still looking back over his shoulder, fearful of what he might see back there catching up with him. His mind gave him no rest. Over and over and over again he saw the blanched face of Cora Haggard. He put his hands over his ears, and still he heard her cry.

Somehow Speck slept, but it was a nervous, threshing sleep. Johnny knew the things that went through Speck's restless dreams. Finally Speck cried out, "No, we didn't mean to!" Johnny reached over and shook him gently. Speck sat bolt upright, blinking in confusion.

"It was a nightmare, Speck. A nightmare, is all."

Speck rubbed his hand over his face and squeezed his eyes shut. "Johnny, I kept seein' her. She just stood there lookin' at me, accusin' me with her eyes, with that blood on her . . . all that blood!"

"Easy, Speck, easy. Lie down and try to sleep some more."

Speck shook his head in misery. "If I got to go

through that every time, I don't think I'll ever want to sleep again."

He got up and rummaged through his warbag. Finding the pistol that had brought on the trouble, he held it a moment, feeling it with the tips of his fingers. Then he drew back and threw it into the river.

He sat on the ground with his knees drawn up and his face buried, and he began quietly crying.

IV

Tired, a separate ache for every long mile, Johnny
felt a lift as the little Fristo ranch headquarters
came in sight along a slow bend in the brush-studded
draw. Stretched out ahead were the corrals he had
helped build as a boy. There was no telling how much
of his own sweat had gone into the slow, laborious
digging of holes, the ditching, the tying together of
cedar stakes, and the tamping of heavy posts to make
the fences bull-stout. He watched the big cypress fan
of the windmill turning slowly in the noonday breeze,
and he wondered how many times he had helped pull
the suckerrods up out of that deep hole.

The first settlers had taken up the river land. Baker
Fristo had arrived a shade late, with little in assets except ambition and a willing back. He had to accept
rangeland away from the living water. But the day of
the windmill had come just in time. He had found that
his land—though there wasn't so much of it—could
produce as much beef as any that lay along the river,
so long as a man had windmills. It didn't matter so
much where the water came from; the main thing was
to have it. He had worked for wages on neighboring
big outfits for cash to buy cattle and drill wells and put
up the wooden towers.

Johnny and Speck rode their flagging horses into
the main waterlot gate. Two high-headed cows with
trailing calves eased warily around them, breaking
into a run when they were in the clear. In front of the
barn the riders climbed down from their saddles, stiff
and groaning from the ache. Pulling off his saddle,

Johnny could tell how badly drawn his horse was. They had put in an awful day yesterday. Without those few hours of rest along the river during the early morning, the horses might not have gotten here. Johnny dropped his saddle front-end down and draped the sweat-soaked blanket across it to dry. He slipped the bridle off the horse's head. The horse turned away and made for the water trough. In a moment Speck's followed suit. Johnny stood wearily with the bridle in his hand, the leather reins trailing on the ground, and watched the thirsty horses drink.

He saw his father walking out from the small frame house, trailed at a respectful distance by a short, dark-skinned Mexican cowboy. Baker Fristo was the picture of Johnny Fristo, plus twenty-five hard years. Grinding work had put a twist in his back, and he walked leaning a little forward. He favored his left leg, an unwanted souvenir from a bronc of years ago. His features were the same as Johnny's but badly abused by time and weather, the hair almost solidly gray now where it showed from beneath his old grease-stained hat. He had a three-day stubble of beard, for his wife lay buried yonder on the hill, and there was no one to tell him to shave.

The ranch was small, and it wasn't much for fancy. But what there was of it, it belonged to him. It had his sweat and blood soaked into it.

He was a plain man, and he showed his emotions. He grabbed Johnny's right hand and clamped his left hand tightly on Johnny's elbow. He squeezed so hard that it hurt. "Son, it's sure good to see you home."

"Howdy, Dad. I'm tickled to be here."

The father squeezed again, and Johnny winced. Baker Fristo stepped back for a long, critical look at his son. He extended his hand to Speck. "Howdy,

Speck. I declare, you fellers look a sight. Bet you
been over in Angelo celebratin' spring. Don't you-all
know when to stop?"

"Mister Fristo, I'm afraid we ain't got nothin' to
celebrate about."

Baker Fristo looked quizzically at his son. His grin
gradually faded. "There's somethin' wrong. What is
it?"

Johnny shook his head and looked at the ground.
"Dad, it's a long story. I don't hardly know where to
start. Reckon we could eat first? We're both hungry
as a wolf."

"Sure. Me and Lalo were just fixin' us some dinner when we saw you-all ride up. We'll throw some
more in the skillet." He studied his son, apprehension
clouding his eyes. "You sure you ain't been drinkin'?"

"No, sir, none atall."

Baker Fristo hesitated, worry still pulling at him as
he looked at the two horses rolling themselves in the
dirt. It was plain that they had been ridden hard.
"Well, let's mosey up to the house." He led the way.
Johnny and Speck trudged along, trying vainly to
keep up with him. Another day, they would have led
him.

When he had finally become financially able, Baker
Fristo had built the frame house to please his wife.
Lord knew, she hadn't had many of the nicer things.
Once it had seemed a big and beautiful thing to
Johnny. Now that he was grown he could see it for the
wooden box that it was. The color was faded and
peeling too. The house hadn't been painted since his
mother passed away. Off to one side of it stood the
picket shack which Baker Fristo had first put up for
his little family so many years ago. It was built of
cedar posts, hewn for a fit and lashed tightly together,

the butt ends set solidly in a trench. The space between the posts had been chinked with plaster. In a way, it resembled a small log cabin standing on end. The Mexican, Lalo Acosta, lived in it now.

Baker Fristo sliced steak from a quarter of tarp-wrapped beef hanging on the small back porch. Because he and the Mexican could not eat a whole beef before it spoiled, it was Baker's custom to pool beeves with several of his neighbors. Johnny stood around hungrily watching the meat frying in the pan. Impatiently he took it out of the skillet before it was completely done. Ordinarily the sight of blood running would make his stomach turn over. Like most Texans, he wanted his beef well done. But he was desperately hungry now, and so was Speck. They took the beef in big bites and ate it quickly, like a pair of starved pups.

The longer he watched them, the more Baker Fristo's eyes narrowed. "You boys are in Dutch, I can tell that."

Johnny glanced at Lalo Acosta, indicating by his expression that he didn't want to talk in front of anybody but his father. "We need a couple of fresh horses, Dad. A couple of good ones."

Baker Fristo understood. "Lalo, how about you goin' out and fetchin' up the horses?"

When the Mexican was gone, Baker Fristo leaned back with his bearded-face long and grave and waited for the story. His jaw hardened as he listened. He blinked faster, the full implication reaching him.

"Poor woman," he said quietly. "No part of it was her fault, but she suffered anyway. Wasn't really your fault either, come right down to it. But you'll be the ones who pay." He placed the palms of his rough hands together and seemed to measure his thick fingers. He glanced at Speck.

"I suppose you went by and told your Aunt Pru?"
Speck nodded.

"What did she say?"

Speck was slow to answer. He got up nervously and paced the floor. "She was awful sorry about it." He looked down. "I reckon I'll go help Lalo."

When Speck was gone, Johnny told his father bitterly about Aunt Pru. "Dad, I never did want to hit a woman in all my life. But I wanted to hit *her*."

Gravely, Baker said, "Son, she can't help bein' what she was born, any more than Speck can. What she's done for Speck she hasn't done out of love. If the truth was known, she likely hates him. But she figures he's her ticket to Heaven. She's figured to buy her way in by feedin' him and bringin' him up, even if she *did* treat him like a dog from the day he was born. Some of what's wrong with Speck today, you can blame on her."

Johnny said, "I'm glad I had you and Mother, and not somebody like *her*."

Baker Fristo looked at his hands again, his jaw quivering. "I've heard of Milam Haggard. I expect most folks have. How long do you think he'll give you?"

"They'll be buryin' her today, I guess. Likely he'll come a-ridin' when the service is over."

"How'll he know where to start lookin'?"

"He can ask the cowboys we've worked with. We didn't make any secret about where we came from, or who our folks was. Who'd have ever thought we'd need to?"

Baker Fristo frowned darkly. "So, he'll likely be stoppin' here about tomorrow. Next day at the latest."

"I expect."

Fristo took a handkerchief from his pocket and blew his nose. He tried to look at Johnny, but he couldn't. He turned and stared out the window awhile. "Johnny, I been doin' a lot of thinkin' lately. I been hopin' you'd get the roamin' out of your system and come home to stay. I need you around here."

"You got Lalo."

"Sure, he's good help but he's not like family. You're all I got left now. I been plannin' how one day soon I'd turn this place over to you. I'll be gettin' too old and stove up. This place would give you a good start. *I* started with nothin'. It's been a hard fight, but at least I've managed to build this little bit. You could build a lot more. You're young yet."

Johnny's throat was tight. "I've missed you, Dad. I've wanted to come home. But first I wanted to prove I could make a hand worth my hire to somebody else. Now I reckon it's too late."

"You could stay and try to talk it out with Haggard."

Johnny shook his head. "You don't know how he looked. If he could have, he'd have killed us and cut us up into little bitty pieces. In his place, I suppose I'd have been the same."

"Once a man starts runnin', it's awful hard to find a stoppin' place, son. He has to keep on runnin' and runnin' till finally he can't run anymore. And in the end he has to turn and face it anyhow."

Johnny's hands shook. "Dad, I just can't face him now. Call me a coward and I guess you'd be right. Maybe someday I can do it. But not now."

Baker Fristo was silent awhile. "It's my fault, in a way. I intended to talk to you but I was afraid you wouldn't listen. Now it's too late."

"Talk about what?"

"About Speck Quitman. I know you like him; *I* like him too. But he's a millstone around your neck."

Johnny stared, wanting to reply but not finding the words.

His father said, "Sure, you made a good pair when you were younger. But you've outgrown him. You're a man now and ready to take on a man's responsibility. Somewhere back yonder, Speck quit growin'. He'll never be a man if he lives to be a hundred."

"Dad . . ."

"Let me finish, son. Some folks say he's simple-minded. I don't go that far. But I *do* say he's got no imagination, no foresight. He's got no idea about the consequences of the things he does. He'd walk into a burnin' house just to get a cigarette lit. Now, that cow trader was the one to blame for what took place yesterday. But think back: if it hadn't been for Speck, it wouldn't have happened, would it?"

Johnny shook his head.

His father went on, "You ought to've said *adiós* to him a long time ago, Johnny. Stay with him and he'll get you killed!"

Johnny nodded a regretful agreement. "You're right, Dad. I've known it a long time. More than once I've started to ride off and leave him someplace, but I never could bring myself to do it. What could he ever do by himself? Now it's too late. Whatever happens to us now, we'll have to face it together."

Baker Fristo brought himself to look at his son, and his wrinkle-edged eyes were sad. Johnny had never seen his father cry but once, that when Mrs. Fristo had died. He thought he could see tears in Baker's eyes now. "Then, son, if there's no other way, you better run. You'll need some money. Whatever I've got, I'll give it to you." He paused. "Any idea where you'll go?"

Johnny shook his head. "West someplace, wherever the trail leads us. Texas is awful big."

Lalo brought in the horses. Badly as he wanted to rest, Johnny knew he and Speck needed to travel all they could. These first days would be crucial. If they could get a long-enough lead on Haggard, there was a chance he never could find them in those vast spaces west of here.

Baker Fristo took a rope out of the barn. He made a gentle underhand loop and caught a long-legged bay. "Speck, here's one that ought to fit you." When Speck bridled the bay and slipped Baker's rope off its neck, Baker reached out and snared a brown. "Johnny, you know this horse, old Traveler. I traded him off of Wilse Arbuckle. He's not much for pretty, but he'll take you all the way and bring you back."

"Thanks, Dad."

They saddled up. Lalo came out from the house with a sack of food—canned goods, cold biscuits, coffee, a little of the beef. Baker Fristo watched while Speck tied the sack on behind his saddle. He shook hands with Speck. "Good luck, boy." He turned back to Johnny. "Write me, son. Let me know you're still alive. Maybe someday I'll be able to tell you it's safe to come back."

Johnny's eyes held doubt. "Dad, we better face what's true. I don't expect I'll ever be able to come back."

Baker Fristo looked down again for a long time. "Well, Johnny, a man does what he has to. Me, I'll just have to give up some dreams. As you get older you find out most of your dreams don't really come true anyway. They keep you goin', but they don't often turn out. Still, without them a man never would amount to much."

Johnny's throat was tight and painful. He wanted to hug his father's neck, the way he had done when he was a boy. But he only gripped Baker's rough hand. "Goodbye, Dad." He swung up into the saddle.

Baker Fristo watched them ride out of sight. Finally, his shoulders slumped helplessly, he turned toward his house, oblivious of Lalo Acosta standing there, sympathy and puzzlement mixed in the Mexican's dark eyes.

"Not goodbye, son. Don't let it be goodbye!"

V

They angled northwestward from the ranch, purposely leaving a clear trail. By and by they came to a public road. They turned into it and stayed long enough to establish an appearance that they intended to remain on it.

Speck seemed numb. He followed along woodenly, doing whatever Johnny did, making no comment, contributing nothing that might help them. At length Johnny said, "We've gone far enough north. There's generally enough horse and wagon traffic on this road to blot out our tracks before long. Maybe by the time Haggard gets to here we'll have him fooled. He'll think we've headed for Colorado City and north."

Speck shrugged as if it didn't matter. "There ain't no use. There ain't nothin' goin' to fool Milam Haggard for long."

"We got to try."

Johnny saw a sandy spot beside the road, and he reined out to the left. "Time we was headin' west, Speck."

Speck only nodded and followed like a pup. Johnny dismounted a hundred feet from the road and handed his reins to Speck. He broke a limb from a mesquite and walked back to the road with it. He carefully brushed out their tracks, eliminating any trace of their having left the road. He moved slowly backward toward the horses, rubbing out all the tracks as he went. From the road there would be no visible sign that anyone had ridden away from it.

"That ought to leave us clear," he said.

Speck's eyes were bleak. "It won't fool him. Ain't nothin' goin' to fool him."

Impatience flared in Johnny. "He's only a man. Any man can be fooled."

"Me and you can. Other folks can. But Haggard can't."

At this point they were nearly thirty miles up the North Concho from San Angelo. They could not follow a route due west from here, for they would not find natural water before they reached the Pecos, not unless it had rained somewhere. And rain in the country west of San Angelo was a thing to be treasured when it came but never to be counted upon. With luck, they might come across a windmill once in a while. Without that luck, they might starve for water before they ever reached the Pecos.

Still, Johnny knew there was a way. If they angled south-westward they would strike the Middle Concho. It meant extra traveling, but it was worth that. The Middle Concho had its beginnings west of San Angelo eighty miles or more, when weather was wet. Chances were right now that its upper reaches would be dry; to be safe, a man had to figure on that. In olden times the wagon trains and trail herds venturing west from Fort Concho had followed along the Middle Concho as far as there was a river. From San Angelo west, the country turned increasingly arid. With every ten miles you could tell a difference. Early travelers had stayed with the living water as long as they could. At best, they knew they faced long, miserable miles of dry travel between the headquarters of the Middle Concho and far-off Horsehead Crossing on the Pecos.

It was foolhardy to start a dry trek any earlier than necessary.

Even now, with windmills increasing over the range, travelers tended to stay with the old trails and the river as long as there was any water in it. It was a conditioning bred into them, like an old-timer watching for Indians long after the last of them were gone.

Johnny and Speck watered the horses in the North Concho beneath the shade of tall old pecan trees whose limbs reached well out over the river. Johnny filled their canteens and listened to the high-pitched hum of the locusts. The afternoon was no more than half gone. If they pushed, they should reach the Middle Concho by dark.

"Speck, you look sick. You feelin' bad?"

"I been feelin' bad ever since that woman died. I'm tired, is all." He grimaced. "Tired. And scared."

"You're not alone, Speck. I'm scared too."

They came upon the river at dusk, and it was time, for both of them were spitting cotton. Johnny rode Traveler over the bank and down to the water. He slid stiffly out of the saddle and loosened the cinch so the horse could drink comfortably. He stepped upstream to the end of the reins, holding them because it was too far from home to let a horse get notions about traveling alone. He dropped on his stomach to drink long and gratefully of the cool water. Finally satisfied, he pushed himself up on one knee and wiped his sleeve across his mouth. Above him, Speck was watering too. The horses were both still drinking.

Johnny called, "Speck, why don't you come down here and drink? The water looks a little clearer."

"It don't matter. I figure on drinkin' it all anyway."

Johnny looked up the river. The stream here was

probably not deep enough to wet a man to his waist, and a good jumper with a running start could almost clear it in a leap. It was a quiet stream most of the time, in summer dropping so low that in places it disappeared below the gravel. But once in a great while its vast dry watershed would catch a whopping big rain that brought water cascading down from the rocky hills and put the Middle Concho up on its hind legs to roar.

Johnny had noticed a bank of dark clouds forming far off in the north the last couple of hours and had made a mental note that they would do to watch. It wasn't considered realistic to predict rain in this part of the country, but it never hurt a man to be prepared.

He glanced again at Speck. "Ain't you ever goin' to get yourself watered out?"

Speck raised up, the water dripping off of his chin. "I never did know just how good water could taste."

"Leave some. We're liable to need it again."

Speck pushed to his feet. It was a considerable effort for him. Johnny could see dark circles under Speck's eyes.

"Speck, we just as well camp here. I'm gettin' hungry."

The Middle Concho lacked the heavy pecan and other timber that the North Concho had. Anyway, if those clouds moved up during the night and brought a spring electrical storm with them, Johnny didn't want to be under a bunch of trees. He'd take his chances with the rain out in the open. He'd seen lightning kill several steers beneath a tree one time. Thing like that came into a man's mind every time he saw a dark cloud.

They took the horses back up the riverbank.

Johnny looked around for dry brush that would make good firewood for camp. He saw some mesquite.

"If you'll get that sack off of your saddle, Speck, I'll start a fire."

Speck turned toward his horse. His face fell in dismay. He glanced at Johnny, unbelieving. "Johnny, that grub ain't here."

Johnny stiffened. "What do you mean, it ain't here?"

"I had it tied to my saddle. Now it's gone."

Johnny swore and looked for himself. "That knot you tied must've come loose. Got any idea where you lost it?"

Impatience had edged into his voice, and Speck reacted with a testy defense. "If I'd known when it come off, I'd have stopped and got it."

Johnny wished he hadn't been so snappish, for he knew the strain Speck had been under. Speck had ridden along so benumbed that he could almost have fallen off the horse and not realized it. Johnny took a long look down their backtrail, what little he could see of it in the growing darkness. "Might've been a mile, or it might've been before we even got out of sight of the North Concho. Cinch we can't go back and hunt for it now."

Speck stared at the saddle as if he couldn't believe it. He reached up and touched the saddlestrings. "We got nothin' to eat. What're we goin' to do?"

"We'll do without."

They staked the horses on the fresh green grass and spread their blankets. Johnny took a hitch in his belt, but it didn't stop his stomach from growling. He looked at Speck with a nagging impatience.

They lay and watched the bullbats swooping down

and touching the river, then lifting and banking around for another try. By and by Speck complained, "Johnny, I sure am hungry."

"Go down there and get you another long drink of water. That'll fill you up."

"I already slosh every time I move."

Gradually, as full darkness came, Johnny grew aware of a pinpoint of light upriver. He narrowed his eyes, wondering. Speck noticed it too.

"Campfire?"

Johnny nodded. "I expect."

Speck pondered awhile in silence. "Reckon they got anything to eat?"

"Sure, they wouldn't be out here without some chuck. But they'd remember us if Milam Haggard came along and asked."

Speck agreed reluctantly. "Still, I can almost smell supper a-cookin'."

"Forget it," Johnny snapped.

Speck was plainly hurt. He sat a long time in brooding silence. "Johnny, I'm a real trial to you."

"Go to sleep, Speck."

"I'm the one caused you all this trouble. Hadn't been for me we'd have somethin' to eat right now. Hadn't been for me, Mrs. Haggard would still be alive. We wouldn't have to be runnin' thisaway." He paused. "You know what you ought to do, Johnny? You ought to just go off and leave me!" He paused again, a long time. Then, worriedly, he said, "You ain't goin' to do it, are you, Johnny? You ain't goin' to go off and leave me?"

The fear in Speck's voice roused pity in Johnny. "No, Speck, I'm not goin' off and leave you."

Johnny turned first one way, then the other on his blanket, trying to find a position where he wouldn't feel the aches and the stiffness. He had to sleep. Hunger teased him, and he tried to force it from his mind. After a long time he drifted into sleep.

With daylight he awoke and looked up into a leaden sky. The smell of rain was fresh in the air. It would be coming down hard before long, he would bet on that.

His stomach growled its hunger. He pushed to his feet and looked around. In the north the sky was a sodden blue. Already raining yonder.

"Speck, we just as well get started."

Speck Quitman stirred and rubbed his eyes. He blinked and looked around sleepily, trying to get his bearings. Speck was always a slow one to wake up. If there had been any nightmares last night, Johnny was not aware of them. He thought Speck probably had been so tired that Mrs. Haggard hadn't entered his mind. That was a good thing, for Speck had come close to breaking down for a while.

Speck looked at the dark sky overhead, then glanced north. "Bad enough just to be hungry. But to be soaked and cold on top of an empty belly is almost too much to stand."

"We got slickers," Johnny said curtly. "At least *those* didn't come loose from the saddles." *There I go*, he thought then, ashamed, *still laying it into him.*

"I know it was my fault," Speck conceded ruefully. "But that don't make it any easier. I'm starvin' to death."

Johnny found himself looking wishfully in the direction where he had spotted the campfire last night. He couldn't find it now in the daylight.

Speck said, "I think we ought to go over yonder and see who them folks are. Maybe it's some ranch's chuckwagon."

"You know the risk."

"And I know I'm so hungry I can't see straight."

Johnny frowned. He had tightened his belt as far as he could pull it, but it hadn't helped much. "All right, let's go."

They saddled up and rode out, following the river. It took a while. There had been no way of telling in the darkness how far away the fire had been, or on which side of the river it lay. It could have been a quarter of a mile or it could have been three times that much. Johnny didn't indulge himself in curiosity. Like Speck, the main thing which bothered him right now was that he was hungry. He looked often at the sky. The rain smell was stronger. It was a bracing smell, one welcomed by a native West Texan under almost any circumstance, for rain came too seldom.

They saw the tent first, then the old Studebaker wagon standing there with a half-wornout wagon-sheet tied loosely over the bows to cover whatever goods were in the wagonbed. Two horses were staked out on grass nearby. A campfire had burned itself down low, a coffeepot sitting on shoveled out coals next to it. Johnny saw several pots and one big Dutch oven, but they looked empty. He wondered if the folks had already eaten, and thrown out what was left.

"Hello," he shouted. "Anybody home?"

It wasn't polite, those days, to ride into someone's camp and not announce yourself.

He saw a flash of skirt at the open tent flap. A girl stepped outside and looked worriedly around. Her gaze fell upon the approaching riders. She lifted her skirts a little and came running. She was young, Johnny saw, maybe seventeen-eighteen. And she was crying.

Speck's horse shied at the flare of skirts rushing straight at him. Johnny's Traveler poked ears forward but didn't otherwise flinch. The girl cried out, "Thank God you've come! Please hurry!" She tried to say more, but her voice broke, and Johnny couldn't understand her. Speck was staring at the girl in total surprise. Johnny swung down. The girl caught his arm and began to pull him toward the camp.

"Please, I've got to have help."

Johnny dragged his feet a little, watching the tent with a considerable degree of suspicion. "Miss, I don't know what your trouble is, but we got trouble too."

With an effort she steadied her voice. "My father's in there. He's dying!"

Johnny glanced back at Speck, who still sat on his horse. "Come on, Speck. We better see what we can do."

Speck frowned. "Johnny, I don't like the smell of this."

"Come on."

Johnny wrapped his reins around a wagonwheel and followed the girl to the tent. A streak of lightning darted to the north, and thunder rolled. A drop of water struck his hand. He paused at the tent flap and looked inside. A man lay on a bedroll spread out on the ground. The hollow-cheeked face was wasted and pale. His beard was the only thing about him that wasn't a liver gray. The man coughed. Reddish foam showed on his lips.

The sight struck Johnny like a blow across the face.

Tuberculosis!

This man was a consumptive. Likely he had come to the dry West Texas region like hundreds of others

from God knew where, hoping this climate would
work the miracle, would bring him a cure. As a boy
Johnny had come upon many of them like this, camped
up and down the rivers, sleeping on the ground, taking their rest, breathing the dry air and praying for
health. Some had found it. Others had found only a
lonely grave, maybe a thousand miles from home.

Johnny knew the girl had judged right. This man
had waited too long.

The girl dropped to her knees and touched a wet
handkerchief to her father's lips. Johnny stared, a
strange knot drawing up inside him. "Is he con-
scious?"

The girl nodded. "Off and on. Right now he knows
I'm here; that's about all. He's going. I can feel it;
he's going." She bit her lip and touched the handkerchief to her father's face again.

Johnny made himself move a little closer, though
a cold chill ran through him. He dreaded this slow,
wasting disease, and he had always avoided people
who had it. "You've known, haven't you, that he
didn't have much time left? You can tell it by lookin'
at him."

She nodded again, dropping her hands to her
knees and staring forlornly into the pale face. "But
they told us this dry air might do it. We hoped so
much, and we came so far. All the way from Illinois."

"You got no other folks here, nobody to help
you?"

"Papa's all I've got left. When he goes . . . there'll
be nobody."

The man coughed again. The girl took one of his
hands and squeezed it helplessly. She looked up, desperate. "Please, he's in pain. Don't you know anything to do for him?"

Regretfully Johnny shook his head. "I never had any experience with this. I don't reckon there's much anybody can do but wait. And maybe pray a little bit."

He didn't think it would be a long wait.

Raindrops began spattering against the canvas. Speck Quitman stepped up to the flap and looked inside suspiciously. His eyes widened. Wordlessly he motioned for Johnny to come outside.

"Johnny, don't you know what the matter is with that man in there? I can tell from here, he's a lunger. Got the lung fever. You better keep out of that tent."

"The girl needs help. He's dyin'."

"He'll take you with him if you catch the lung fever. Let's get the hell out of here!"

"Speck, she needs help."

"What can you do? Can you stop him from dyin'?"

"No, but somebody ought to be here. She'll be alone."

"She's no concern of ours. She was alone before we come here. We could as easy of rode on by, and she'd be no worse off than she ever was."

Johnny didn't know what it was about the girl that had struck him so. "I can't do it, Speck. She's got too much trouble for a girl like her to handle alone."

"We got trouble too."

The girl called from the tent, "Mister! Oh, Mister!"

Johnny turned and left Speck standing there. The man was coughing again, harder than before. The girl was talking quietly, trying to hold down panic. "It's all right, Papa. We've got some help. It's all right, Papa."

Johnny knelt helplessly, knowing there wasn't a thing he could do but sympathize.

The man's eyes opened a little. He blinked, trying to focus. He looked a moment at the girl, then weakly turned his head to look at Johnny. His voice was only a whisper. "Who are you?"

"Name's Johnny Fristo, sir."

"You help . . . help my daughter. Help her."

"I'll help her."

"Please . . . don't leave her."

Johnny swallowed. He found himself making a promise he knew he couldn't keep. "No, sir, I won't leave her."

The dying man lapsed back into the shadows. There was no sound except his ragged breathing and the quiet sobbing of the girl. That, and the rain drumming down on the tent.

Rain! And Speck was out there in it! Johnny eased to the tent flap and looked outside. He saw that Speck had unsaddled their horses and shoved the saddles into the wagon. Speck squatted beneath the vehicle, his yellow slicker wrapped around him, vainly trying to keep dry. There was enough wind with the rain that the water drove in under the wagon.

"Speck, you come in here before you get yourself soaked."

Speck was resolute. "No! I'd rather take my chances with the rain. If you had any smart you'd be out here too."

Johnny shivered, for this was a cold rain, the kind that reminds you it hasn't been long since winter. It was the kind that sometimes caught fresh-sheared sheep and chilled them to death. But he could tell Speck wouldn't come into the tent.

"At least get into the wagon before you get soaked any worse."

He turned back to the girl and wished again he

could do something besides just stand here and watch. When you came right down to it, there wasn't much anybody could have done now, not even a doctor. Just wait. So he waited. And at last death came quietly into the tent, touched the girl's father and peacefully took him away. It was hard to tell just when sleep lapsed over into death.

Or, Johnny wondered, was there really much difference?

VI

The girl cried softly. Johnny put his hands on her shoulders. He thought he probably should say something, but nothing came to mind, so he let it go. All he could give her was sympathy, and he couldn't put even that into words.

The rain stopped. Johnny walked out of the tent and raised his head. For a moment the sun broke through, and it struck the spot along the river where the camp stood. He looked up through the small break, and the sun struck him full in the eyes. A chill passed through him. He had always taken his Bible teachings literally, and he wondered if there was some special meaning in the way the light touched here, where a man had just died.

It came to him that this was the second death he had witnessed in three days, and he shivered again.

Back in the tent, he found the girl was no longer crying. She still knelt, solemnly looking down at her father.

Johnny said, "I expect you'll be wantin' to take him back to Angelo."

The girl was a long time in replying. "We didn't know anybody in San Angelo. We just came there on the train, and we bought this old wagon and team at a stable. We came on out because Papa thought camping on the ground would cure him."

"Seems like you came an awful long way."

"We stopped once closer in, but the man who owned the land didn't want us there. He made us move. We came here, and nobody has bothered us."

She paused. "Besides, I don't have money left to bury him with. It took about all we had to get him here."

"You got to do somethin' about him."

"I know. He liked this spot. It seemed to strike his fancy the minute he saw it. I think he would have liked to be buried here."

Johnny rubbed his neck, considering. Seemed to him he'd heard that when somebody died you had to report it to the law, get death papers and such. Just to bury a man out here this way might have been all right ten or fifteen years ago, but now it was probably against the law. It was too simple to be legal anymore.

But, on the other hand, it would be a minor thing compared to the trouble he and Speck were already in.

The girl's eyes pleaded. "Will you help me?"

He couldn't have turned her down if he had seen Milam Haggard and a big posse come riding over the hill.

"We'll help you." He looked outside at the gray sky. "It might set in to rainin' again directly. I expect if we're goin' to dig, we better get at it."

He went out and looked around for a pick and shovel. He found Speck standing by the wagon, his clothes wet. "Speck, I swear you look a sight. You ought to've come inside like I told you."

Speck shook his head. "You about ready to leave here now?"

At another time Johnny might have smiled, for it struck him a little funny how Speck had lost his concern over being hungry. "Speck, her father died. We're goin' to bury him before we go."

Speck's mouth dropped open. "Johnny, we got to be a-ridin'. Haggard is liable to be most any place."

"We can't just leave this girl here with a dead body on her hands. We got to help her."

Speck looked for a moment as if he had about as soon fight as argue. But he gave in. "All right, sooner we get it done the sooner we get movin'. I'll dig, but I ain't goin' to handle him none, you understand?" He was about to say something else, but he sneezed.

Johnny said, "You oughtn't to be in those wet clothes. Maybe the girl can lend you somethin' of her dad's."

Speck shook his head violently. "No, sir, thank you, I wouldn't touch it." He took the shovel from Johnny's hand.

They let the girl pick the spot, back away from the river where no flood would disturb the grave.

That was the first time Johnny mentioned to her that they were hungry. She nodded solemnly. "I'm sorry. I should've asked you a long time ago."

"You had aplenty to worry about."

"I should've asked you anyway. I'll go fix something."

Speck started the digging. Johnny walked down to the camp with the girl. In the wagonbed he found a small supply of dry wood. She had been farsighted enough to put it under there before the rain started. In a wooden box were some canned goods, coffee, flour and sundry camp supplies. He put some of the dry wood into the firepit, poured a little kerosene over it and set it ablaze. He could see the girl through the open tent flap. She was pulling the blanket up over her father's face. Johnny turned away, respecting her privacy.

"Need any more help right now?" he asked when she came out.

"I'll be all right."

"I best go help my partner."

She said worriedly, "He's wet. I could get some of Papa's dry clothes for him."

"He wouldn't wear them. He takes some funny notions sometimes. But I'll tell him you made the offer, and thanks."

He had been looking around camp for something that would do as a headboard. All he could find was the endgate from the wagon. He took it out.

"Funny," he remarked, "I don't even know what name to put on this."

A tear started down her cheek. "His name was Edward Barnett."

"I never did hear yours, either."

"Mine is Tessie. Tessie Barnett."

With a rope Johnny and Speck lowered Edward Barnett into the grave. They stood and looked at the ground while the girl started reading the Twenty-third Psalm in a weak, strained voice. She finally broke down. Johnny took the Bible from her hands. He finished reading what she had started. Done, he added the one thing he could remember from funerals he had attended: "The Lord giveth, and the Lord taketh away. Blessed be the name of the Lord." He closed the Book and handed it to her.

She glanced up at him, and their eyes held a moment. Something stirred Johnny, something he had never felt before.

"Thank you," she said. She turned and walked back down to camp.

Speck and Johnny filled the grave and put the headboard in place, bracing it with rocks to make sure it didn't fall down. Speck said, "Reckon anybody'll ever notice it up here? It's a ways off of the trail."

"I don't know. Maybe they won't. But it don't seem right to put a man away and not even leave a headboard to mark his passin'. Man ought to have at least that much to show that he once walked this earth. Else he'd just as well never have been here."

Speck shrugged. "Don't look like he's left much to show for him. An old wagon, a tent. Ain't much to make a man's whole life look worthwhile."

Down the slope, the girl was breaking camp. Johnny said, "Maybe it's not the money and the property a man leaves that's really important, Speck. They get scattered, and who's ever goin' to remember him by that? But he left that girl. She'll remember him as long as she lives. She'll have children someday, and she'll tell them about him. They'll remember. Come right down to it, Speck, I don't guess a marker is really so important after all."

They folded the tent and placed it in the wagon. Speck went out and got the team. Johnny looked worriedly at the girl. "Miss, what're you goin' to do now?"

She didn't look at him. "I don't know. I hadn't let myself think about it. I just know I can't stay here where he died."

"You can sell the wagon and team, I suppose, and go back where you came from."

"I've got no family there anymore. There's nothing to go back to."

"Then maybe San Angelo. It's a good-sized town. I expect a girl like you could get decent work there."

She nodded. He could still see a trace of tears in her eyes. She had a lost look about her. She was young yet to be alone like this, to be left a stranger bewildered in a land that was alien to her, a land where she knew not a single soul.

"I have to live somewhere." She squared her shoulders, forcing herself to take courage. "How far is it to San Angelo?"

"A fair piece. Forty miles, I expect." He looked at

her with worry. "Think you can make it there by yourself?"

She was plainly dubious. "I guess I could." She bit her lip. "Do you suppose . . . do you suppose I could get you fellows to go with me? I've never been by myself like this." She looked away as if ashamed. "I guess I'm scared."

Johnny saw alarm surge into Speck's face, and he moved to head Speck off. "Miss Barnett, we're goin' west. We can't go to San Angelo."

"I don't have much money left, but I'll give you what I *do* have."

"It ain't the money. I mean, if we could do it atall, we'd do it for nothin'. But you see . . . well, the truth is we *can't* go back. They're lookin' for us there."

She slowly shook her head. "I can't believe that. You've been kind to me, both of you. You couldn't have done anything bad."

Johnny couldn't hold his gaze to hers. "We did a bad thing, but not on purpose. It was an accident." He didn't want to tell her more than that. He was glad she didn't ask.

Speck's calmness even surprised Johnny. Speck spoke to the girl in a gentle voice. "We'll hitch up your horses, Miss. Too bad we can't do more." It didn't take Johnny long to figure out that Speck was simply glad to be shed of her and get moving again.

They turned the wagon around for her and headed it eastward, toward San Angelo. The girl said tightly, "Thank you again, both of you. I'll never forget this."

Johnny said, "I wish you would. I mean, if any-body asks you . . ."

"I won't say a thing."

They sat and watched her start. They watched her top out over the hill, a tiny-looking thing and all alone.

Speck wondered, "Johnny, reckon she'll ever make it there all by herself?"

"I don't know. I purely don't know."

"It's a long ways."

Johnny kept watching the girl, and that strange feeling came over him again. Suddenly he touched spurs to his horse. "Come on, Speck, we're not goin' to let her do it."

"What can we do? We can't go with her."

"We can take her west with us a ways. There's bound to be a ranch up here someplace where we can leave her with folks who'll see she gets to town all right."

"Johnny, I do believe you're losin' your head over that girl."

"I just never could sleep, wonderin' if she ever got there all right or if somethin' happened to her. Come on, Speck."

Speck grumbled, but he accepted the inevitable and followed.

VII

Milam Haggard was tired, but he had cultivated a rigid self-discipline that would not allow him to show it. Riding a black-legged dun, leading a brown horse with a small pack, he kept his back straight, his shoulders high. His flat-brimmed black hat with the round crown was pulled down low over his eyes, so that he held his chin high to be able to see out under the brim. It gave him the appearance of a man with strong pride, and the appearance was not misleading. But it was not pride which dominated him now. He burned with a grim and silent determination.

He had passed the North Concho village of Water Valley a while ago, and ahead of him lay the Baker Fristo place. He had made some inquiry around San Angelo about this Fristo. Most people had told him Fristo was a hard-working small cowman who had pulled himself up by his own bootstraps and never made trouble for anybody. But Haggard knew circumstances could forge drastic changes in a person. The mildest of men would stand up and fight for a son.

He was sure the situation here would be different from the one he had stepped into in San Angelo when he visited Speck Quitman's aunt. She had broken into uncontrollable hysterics and had cried about the shame that had been brought upon her. It had seemed to Haggard that she showed little concern for her nephew but a great deal about the disgrace that had befallen her good family name.

Haggard had held her in contempt, but he had

stayed until he found out that the two cowboys were likely to visit Baker Fristo. Fristo probably wouldn't tell him anything on purpose, Haggard knew. But long ago he had learned that people would usually tell more than they realized, more than they intended. A word, a glance, a set of tracks—and he might discover all he really needed to know.

Haggard rode out of the brushy draw and saw before him the big windmill, the rambling set of corrals, the barn, the fading frame house. He reined up for a long, careful look around. He studied closely the places where a man or men could hide—behind the barn, the house, a stack of unused cedar posts, a pile of barbed-wire rolls. Some of these he carefully eliminated one by one, concentrating on their shadows until he was sure nothing stood behind them that didn't belong. Still, plenty of dangerous places were left. He drew the saddlegun up out of its scabbard, laid it across his lap and gently touched spurs to the dun. He moved forward in a slow walk, watching with the tense care of a man who half expects to be shot out of the saddle.

He heard talk. His gaze caught movement out in one of the corrals. Two men were hanging a new wooden gate. Haggard lightly touched the reins and moved the dun in that direction, the pack horse following. He noted that the man facing him was a Mexican. That checked with what Haggard had been careful to find out. Fristo had one man living on the ranch with him, a hired Mexican.

The Mexican spoke quietly. The other man turned to squint at Haggard. The man made a move with his hand, and Haggard's grip tightened on the saddlegun. But he saw then that the man was only wiping sweat from his dusty face.

Now Haggard could see the face, and he knew this was Baker Fristo. He had seen Johnny Fristo once on the street of Sonora and again a few minutes the day of Cora Haggard's death. That face would be burned into his memory to the last day Haggard lived. This was the same face, except for the many extra years to which the deep furrows testified.

"Howdy," Fristo said. He was not unfriendly. "Git down and rest yourself."

Haggard did not do so immediately. He sat still, his gaze sweeping the corrals, the barn.

Fristo understood. "You can quit lookin'. Ain't nobody here but us, just me and Lalo. Nobody else."

Haggard glanced at the Mexican and saw apprehension in the dark eyes. For a little of nothing, the man would turn and run like a deer.

Fristo said, "I ain't lyin' to you, Mister Haggard."

Haggard let his surprise show a little. "You know me?"

"Never met you, but I know who you are. I know why you've come. My boy's not here. Even if he was, he wouldn't shoot you in the back. He ain't that sort."

Haggard stared at Fristo and then looked around for sign of a gun somewhere. Fristo said, "No guns. Me and Lalo, we're just workin' on the corrals a little. We didn't figure on shootin' anybody."

Pointedly Haggard said, "If you know why I've come here, you might be inclined to shoot *me*."

Fristo shook his head. "I'd rather just talk to you, Mister Haggard."

"Talk won't change anything. You ought to know that."

"I always heard you were a reasonable man, Mister Haggard. I think the truth would change things, if you'd just listen to it."

Haggard made no reply. Fristo gave up waiting for one. "Well, no use us standin' out here in the hot sun. It's dinnertime directly, and I'd just as well go fix us somethin' to eat. You'll stay and eat with us, won't you, Mister Haggard?"

Surprised, Haggard said, "You're askin' *me* to eat with you?"

"It's dinnertime. Nobody ever left my place hungry."

"I've come here lookin' for your boy. And you know why."

Fristo nodded slowly. "I know. I aim to try and talk you out of it."

"It won't work."

"I'll try anyway. You got to stop and eat sometime. You'd just as well do it here."

Haggard stepped to the ground frowning, studying this bent man. He couldn't remember that he had ever run into a situation like this. In a different way it bothered him as badly as his encounter with that wailing aunt. He stopped at a trough near the windmill and let the horses water. Then he followed Fristo to the frame house. He glanced for a moment at the old picket shack nearby. The thought struck him that the two young men he sought could be holed up in there. But instinctively he knew Fristo wasn't lying to him. The pair had gone.

On the front porch Fristo nodded toward a washstand on which were a bucket of water, a dipper and a washpan. "I expect you're pretty hot and dusty, Mister Haggard. Probably make you feel better to wash yourself."

As the guest, Haggard washed first, then Fristo. In the house Fristo motioned toward a rocking chair. "Set yourself a spell while I see what I can fix."

Waiting, Haggard looked around. One thing he saw was an old wedding picture. Baker Fristo in that picture was the image of his son today. Plainly enough, a woman had lived here once. Just as plainly, she had been gone a long time. The curtains on the windows were gray now with dust and smoke. A woman had put them there, but a woman would not have allowed them to get in that condition. The dishes on the shelf bore a nice pattern and showed a woman's touch. But some were chipped at the edges, the result of a man's rougher handling. Haggard noted that far fewer cups were left than plates of the original set. Several plain white cups had been added to take the place of some broken by inveterate male coffee drinkers.

It did not escape his notice that when the leftover morning coffee was hot, Baker Fristo passed up the nicer cups and purposely took out one of the plain kind for his own use. He was evidently more comfortable with those.

I guess I would be too, Haggard thought.

He wouldn't have admitted it to anybody, but the thought of settling down and living with Cora had almost frightened him. He had lived alone a long time, Haggard had. He had lived a harsh, womanless life on the trail and in small one-room shacks in a dozen towns. He had been comfortable in austerity. Often he had wondered how he was going to reconcile himself to the change a man had to make when he married, especially when he married a lady of Cora's kind. He would not have asked Cora to compromise her ways. The adjustment would have had to be his. Sometimes he had lain awake at night wondering how and if he could actually make a success of it.

Now he would never know. He and Cora had never had much chance to find a life together.

Baker Fristo broke into Haggard's line of thought. "Afraid my cookin' ain't much for fancy, but it fills in between the ribs. It's on."

Haggard moved to the table. He had never really been hungry. He had never been one to eat much. Since his wife's death, eating had been a necessity that he forced upon himself.

The Mexican came in and sat at the table with them. Haggard noticed this. He had been at many places where it wouldn't have been done. Haggard ate slowly, forcing the food down because he knew he needed it. Fristo ate in silence, but Haggard could feel the man's eyes appraising him. Haggard found himself liking the man. It would have been easier if he hadn't.

Fristo finished eating and leaned back in his chair, his eyes steady on Haggard. "It's a hard and bitter thing for a man to lose his wife. I know, because I've been there."

Haggard was slow to answer. "Then you'll understand how I feel, and why I do what I do."

"Those boys had no thought of hurtin' your wife. If it had even occurred to them that a thing like that could happen, they wouldn't have stopped the hack. But they figured they'd been done wrong, just the way you feel you've been wronged. They made a mistake, like you're fixin' to. They'll regret it as long as they live. So will you, Mister Haggard, if you go through with this."

"They killed her. All the talk in the world won't change that."

"It was an accident. The blame isn't all theirs. It wasn't even them that fired the gun; it was that feller named Larramore."

"*They* told you that, Fristo. You can't really know."

"My boy told me, and he's never lied."

"He never killed anybody before, either."

"They're just boys, Haggard."

"They're men. They're both of age, and that makes them men in the sight of the law."

"And where *is* the law, Haggard? How come it's not with you, helpin' you hunt them?"

Haggard looked across the room, his jaw ridged in anger. "The law looked at it the way you do. The sheriff down there, he said it was an accident. He wouldn't file a murder charge. But she's dead. Nothing anybody says can bring her back."

"And killin' my son—will *that* bring her back?"

"He killed her, he and that other one. An eye for an eye is what the Bible says. It's God's vengeance!"

"God also has His mercy."

Helpless anger simmered in Haggard. He couldn't sit there and argue over this thing as if it were a cow trade or something. His wife was dead. The grief and the anger were still sharp and bitter, cutting through him like a knife. He pushed to his feet. "I'll be ridin' on. I'm sorry I stopped here."

Baker Fristo stood up too. "Please, Haggard, listen to me. Think!"

"I've *been* thinkin'. That's all I've done for days. I've hardly even slept for the thinkin' I've done. And it always comes back to the same thing: they killed my wife. I'm goin' to get them, Fristo. And the only thing I'll be sorry for is that it's *your* son."

He turned and started for the front door. He heard Baker Fristo move quickly. Instinctively Haggard stopped. Even as he turned back, his hand darted downward, coming up with the pistol from his hip.

Baker Fristo had lifted a rifle from a set of hooks on the wall and was starting to turn with it.

Haggard thumbed back the hammer of the pistol. "Stop it! Stop it right there!" Fristo hesitated a second, then kept on turning, the rifle still in his hands.

Haggard cried, "Stop it, Fristo! You haven't got a chance! For God's sake, man, I don't want to kill you!"

Fristo froze, but he still held the rifle. Eyes desperate, he looked into the bore of Haggard's pistol. The color began leaving his face. The man was scared. But Haggard could tell he was also determined, and that made him dangerous.

Fristo said, "You'll kill me, but I'll kill you too, Haggard."

"Not a chance. It's not worth the try."

"My son's life is worth *any* chance."

"You haven't *got* any chance," Haggard repeated firmly. "I'd put a bullet through your heart, and you couldn't pull that trigger. But I don't want to do it. Believe me, I don't want to do it." He waited for sign Fristo was going to relent. "Put it down now, Fristo. For God's sake, put it down!"

He could see the realization of helplessness slowly come into Fristo's eyes. And with the helplessness, a glistening of tears.

Fristo laid the rifle on the floor and stood up, his shoulders slumped, his face stamped with defeat. He looked like an old man. "I tried. I tried."

Haggard found his heart was beating rapidly. He had come within an inch of having to kill this man. It was a killing he would have regretted as long as he lived. "You've got a lot of guts, Mister Fristo. If it's any consolation to you, you can always tell yourself you did what you could. But you never had a chance, not from the first."

"It's not important that I *tried*. What matters is that I failed. And now you'll go on out and kill my son."

Haggard swallowed. He saw the Mexican come up beside Fristo, the fear somehow gone from him. He saw the intention written all across the little man's dark face.

"Don't try it, *hombre*. You just leave that gun lay there or I'll have to kill you."

Lalo slowly backed away. Haggard picked up the rifle. He unloaded it, carefully watching the two men. He started to lay the rifle across a chair, then changed his mind. "I'll take this with me out to the barn and leave it there. I'd be real glad if you-all would just stay here till I get out of sight."

He could see desperation clutching at Fristo. "You can't find them, Haggard. It's two thousand miles from here to the Canada border. They could be any place."

"You mean they went north?"

Fristo nodded, and Haggard felt somehow a little sorry for him. It was a transparent effort, born of unreasoning desperation. Had the pair *really* gone north, not even an Indian torture would have made Fristo admit it.

Haggard knew within reason they wouldn't go south again; that was where they had come from. Nobody here ever ran east, back into the settled country where it would be easy to locate them. Only one way was left: west. Anybody going west from here would almost surely strike for the Middle Concho, Centralia Draw and ultimately Horsehead Crossing on the Pecos. That narrowed it, made it easier for him.

He said, "Mister Fristo, I'm sorry for you." Then he left.

VIII

It was night now, and the storm was coming back. Johnny and Speck sat beside the wagon, watching jagged fingers of lightning shatter the black sky to the south. Short flashes illuminated the underside of ugly clouds that likely were carrying hail. Thunder rolled gradually closer, and the ground trembled.

Speck's cold was settling deeper in his chest. Johnny could hear it when Speck coughed. That was more and more often.

"Sure fixin' to rain again directly," Johnny remarked, watching the sodden clouds. "I reckon we best sleep in the wagonbed, under the sheet."

The campfire had burned down low, but in its dim glow Johnny could see the girl seated in front of her tent, staring sadly into the coals.

Speck's voice was coarsening from his cold. "Johnny, that girl is slowin' us down somethin' awful."

"We can't just ride off and leave her."

"There's some as would."

"We're bound to find a ranchhouse someplace tomorrow."

Speck didn't look at Johnny. "Kind of got you goin', ain't she?"

Johnny hadn't realized it showed. "Worried about her, is all. Things could happen to a girl out here like this."

"Get all wrapped up in a girl and you'll forget your old partner, that's what you'll do." Johnny wondered if he detected a vague resentment. Speck added, "If she was some middle-aged old maid, reckon you'd be as worried about her?"

Johnny didn't reply to that. He was afraid he knew the answer, and it didn't make him particularly proud.

Speck began coughing again. It shut him up, and Johnny was not sorry. He didn't feel like arguing. He pushed to his feet and walked down to the tent. The girl didn't seem to notice him at first. Her gaze was fixed on the glowing coals.

"Anything we can do for you, Miss Barnett?"

Startled, she glanced up. "No, thank you. I'm afraid the only thing that will help me now is time . . . lots of time."

"You'll just hurt yourself, broodin' thisaway."

"Not easy to put a thing like this out of your mind, though, especially as fresh as it is. I'm not sure I want to, not for a while yet." She looked back at the coals. "I'm sorry to be a burden to you."

"You're no burden."

"I'm keeping you here."

"We'll be all right."

"Will you? What about the man you said is after you?"

"Rain this mornin' washed out all the tracks we made up to the time we struck your camp. Rain again tonight will wash out what we've made today. I expect he'll be hard put to follow us."

That wasn't the whole truth, and he knew it. But he saw no gain in telling her Milam Haggard would follow the river, same as they were doing. It was the natural thing. Speck hadn't mentioned it, either, and Johnny hoped it hadn't occurred to him.

The girl stared into the dying campfire. The smell

of burning mesquite blended well with the clean smell of oncoming rain. She said, "My father always liked the rain. Said it seemed to wash the world down and give it a fresh start. Said it needed a clean start as often as it could get one."

Johnny nodded gravely. "I wish *I* could get a clean start." He hadn't meant to say anything. But it came to him that if the girl could find concern for someone else's troubles, she might for at least a while forget her own.

Her eyes were sympathetic. "Can't you?"

He shook his head. "It'll take a lot more than rain to wash away what happened." To suit Milam Haggard, it was going to take *blood*.

"Do you have any folks, Johnny?"

"My dad, is all. And I've said goodbye to *him*. Way things are, I doubt I'll ever get to see him again."

"Then you must feel a little like I do." The cool wind came, and she shivered. "It almost makes you panic to realize all of a sudden that you're alone. Deep down, you know the pain will pass someday. But that doesn't help much right now."

Kneeling beside her, Johnny picked up a stick and idly poked at the coals. "I'll tell you somethin' my dad said when my mother died. It helped me. He said to look forward, try and put yourself into the future. He said imagine it's been a long time, that whatever has hurt you is in the past and the healin' already done. He said you know that someday it'll be like that, so try to pretend now that someday has already come."

"Does it work?"

"It helps. It's a way to borrow strength and ease the pain. Eventually you find that someday *has* come. It's over, and you've lived." He paused, solemn. "I've used it a right smart the last couple of days. Lord knows, a man needs anything he can find that'll help, even a little."

She sat awhile in a dark silence. "Your dad must be a good man."

"The best there is."

She brought her gaze up to his face. "And he raised a son just like him."

They were traveling again by shortly after daylight, the wagon wheels cutting deep into the mud of last night's rain. Turning in the saddle, Johnny worriedly studied the bold tracks they were leaving. A blind mule could follow them. Moreover, when the ruts dried they would set, a little like concrete. They would be a long time in eroding away.

Of course, Haggard probably wouldn't know the cowboys were traveling with a wagon. But their own horses were leaving tracks too. By this time Haggard no doubt had studied the tracks until he could pick these two horses out of a remuda by them. For a little while Johnny and Speck tried riding ahead of the wagon, hoping the girl's team would wipe out their tracks. It didn't work very well, and they quit trying. Johnny doubted an expert tracker like the manhunter Haggard would be fooled very long.

Nothing to do, then, but try to find a ranch where they could leave the girl, then pick up speed as they rode on west. Out there it never rained much. The constant wind would worry away at a set of tracks in soft earth until they were gone within hours.

They traveled all morning along the trace started by the Butterfield stages and followed since by thousands of wagons over the long frontier years. With the warmth of the bright morning sun, the moisture from the rain began to evaporate. The steam of it set Johnny to sweating. For Speck it was even worse. His face was flushed. He wouldn't let Johnny touch him, but Johnny knew his partner was beginning to run a fever of sorts. Speck's eyes were red, his temper short. Times like this, Johnny had found it best simply to leave him alone.

They stopped to eat a little and rest the horses. Speck was in misery, both of body and of soul. Sweat soaked his cotton shirt as he sat in the thin shade of a big mesquite. His eyes were riveted to the backtrail. It was easy to read his mind. He ate little.

"Johnny, I'm afraid I caught the lung fever."

"Where'd you get a notion like that? It takes a long time to develop the lung fever. You took yourself a cold out in the rain, that's all."

Speck nibbled at hope, though unconvinced. "You reckon that's it?"

"Sure, you'll be all right. But you need to rest awhile. Soon as we find a ranchhouse."

"We done rested too much now. Old Haggard is liable to come a-ridin' along most any minute now."

Johnny shook his head. "Not yet. He hasn't had time."

"He don't need time. He'll smell us out like a bloodhound. We need to keep on a-movin'."

"Even horses have to have rest. Here, Speck, eat a little more."

Speck waved food away. The melancholy came over him again. "You're wrong, Johnny. It *is* the lung fever. I caught it off of that girl's daddy as sure as sin."

Johnny didn't feel like going through the whole argument again, so he let it lie. Before long he was itching to go, even as he knew Speck was. Though reason told him Haggard was still well behind, the thought of the man raised something more than physical fear. The ex-Ranger's reputation was awesome. It was easy to believe somehow that Haggard stood eight feet tall, that he did, indeed, have the bloodhound's gift of scent, that with only a look he put the mark of death on a man.

A chill ran through Johnny, and he said, "Let's go, Speck."

About the middle of the afternoon they saw a trace leading off to the northwest, a faint wagon trail that had been used only enough to show it belonged to somebody. Johnny glanced back at the lagging Speck, hunched in the saddle. He pulled out into the faintly marked trail and motioned for Tessie Barnett to bring her wagon along.

Speck drew over to the side of the trail, his head down. He had nothing to say. Johnny edged his horse back beside the wagon. "Tessie . . . Miss Barnett, here's a trail. Chances are it leads to a ranch yonderway someplace. Not a big outfit, from the looks of the trail. But a ranch, anyway." He looked into her eyes, and he couldn't tell for sure whether she was glad or not. He got an odd feeling that she wasn't, really.

"Think it'll be far, Johnny?"

"No way of tellin'. We'll know when we come to it."

She glanced at Speck. "He's pretty sick. He'd be better off in the wagon."

Johnny frowned. "I expect he would." He looked toward Speck. "Why don't you sit up here with Miss Barnett? I'll tie your horse on behind."

Speck didn't argue. Johnny gave him a boost up, and he could tell Speck needed it. He couldn't have made the climb by himself. "Speck, when we find a ranchhouse, you're goin' to have to rest a spell, and no buts about it."

Speck gritted miserably, "Let's just be a-gettin' on."

They rode an hour, following the dim trail over rocky hills and through dry-looking scrub cedar timber. It hadn't rained so much here. Down yonder from the trail ran a small creek that would empty into the Middle Concho somewhere to the south. Finally, as Johnny was beginning to wonder if the trail really led anywhere, they came upon a ranch headquarters. It sat at the foot of a hill, with chinaberry trees rimming what appeared to be a small seep or spring. For a moment Johnny's spirit sagged. He had hoped for more. This was just a little box house—a one-room affair likely, or two rooms at the most. A small rock shed served as saddle house and barn. A couple of weathered brush arbors out by the shed had been intended orginally to shade the livestock. But they hadn't been kept up, and much of the brush topping had fallen to the ground, leaving big openings for the sun to shine through.

Another brush arbor stood in front of the unpainted frame house. Beneath it a lone man sat in an old rocking chair.

The thought came to Johnny that this was no time of day for a man to be lazing around the house. He ought to be out tending to work. At least, that was the way his dad had taught him. But he knew not all people looked at life that way. From the rundown appearance of the place, Johnny would bet this man spent far more time under the shady arbor than at work out in the sun.

The man stopped rocking and sat motionless,

watching their approach. Nearing, Johnny saw that this was a man of forty or so, running strongly to paunch. His hair was starting to gray in spots, and he hadn't shaved in a week or two. His clothes would have stood alone if he had taken them off, which he probably hadn't done in days. He gave no sign that he was glad to see company.

"You-all lost or somethin'?" He said it to Johnny, but his gaze quickly shifted to the girl. Lazily he stood up.

Johnny eyed him closely. "You got some drinkin' water?"

The man jerked this thumb toward the house. "Back there in the cistern." He didn't move to fetch any.

Johnny said, "We been lookin' a long time for a ranchhouse. This girl needs help to get back to San Angelo."

The man looked Johnny up and down. "You look to me like a healthy feller. I doubt there's anything she needs that you couldn't of give her." He stepped out from under the arbor and squinted in the sun, looking closer at the girl. "Been a long time since there was any woman at this place. If I'd of knowed you was comin', I'd of shaved and fixed up a little." His gaze fell on Speck. "You look like you'd fell off the wagon and got run over. What's the matter with *you*?"

Johnny answered for Speck. "He's sick. Got wet and took a bad cold. I was hopin' he could rest here a little."

The man frowned, still not friendly. "Sick folks take a lot of carin' for. I don't have much time."

"You won't have to do anything. We'll do it."

"I got mighty little room here, as you can see. I reckon you could roll him out a blanket under the arbor, though. Don't see how that could hurt nothin'."

Johnny felt anger rising. This was a country where most people were openhanded and ready to help, for company was scarce and friendships prized like coin of the realm. In his limited travels Johnny hadn't run into many like this before. This was an attitude alien to the time and the country. "Thanks," he said dryly. "Thanks a lot."

The man looked at Tessie again. "You said somethin' about the girl needin' somebody to help her get back to Angelo."

"I was sort of hopin' there would be somebody here who could take her."

"Ain't nobody here but me."

"Any neighbors?"

"Not for a long ways. I never did care much for neighbors anyhow. Always come a-borrowin' or wantin' help. And then they're always accusin' you of this, that, and the other." He studied the girl, then turned back suspiciously to Johnny. "How come you don't take her to Angelo yourself?" When Johnny didn't answer, realization came into the man's muddy eyes. "You boys are on the dodge, that's what it is. I can tell."

Johnny swallowed. It occurred to him that this man might try to hold them in hope of a reward. He glanced around quickly for sign of a gun. He saw none.

The man looked at Speck. "Maybe he didn't catch cold atall. Maybe he's wounded."

Johnny said, "He's not wounded. I told you the truth."

"Who did you fellers rob? A bank? The Santy Fee railroad?"

"We never robbed anybody."

"Then you *killed* somebody. That's what you done, you killed somebody!"

Guilt rose hotly to Johnny's face. The girl spoke up. "They didn't kill anybody. They were there, but that was all. They weren't the ones who did it."

Johnny said, "Hush, Tessie."

The man stared at her. "How did you fit into this, girl? You look a mite green to be runnin' with the wild bunch."

Johnny protested, "We told you the truth. We found her along the trail. Her daddy was sick. He died and we buried him. Now we're just lookin' for somebody to take her to Angelo. We couldn't go off and leave her there."

The man's gaze moved to first one then the other, calculating. Mostly he looked at the girl. "I don't want to get in Dutch with the law. I can't go harborin' no fugitives. You boys can water your horses and get a drink for yourselves. Then you got to get off of my place. The girl, if she wants to, can stay here. I'll see she gets to Angelo."

Johnny pointed to Speck. "Mister, my partner's sick."

"He'll be dead if the law finds him here. I don't want him on my place."

Angrily Johnny tried to stare him down. But the man simply ignored him and turned back to the girl. "Honey, if you want to get down from that wagon . . ."

Tessie Barnett looked at Johnny. "I don't know . . ."

Johnny stepped closer to her. "I don't like the looks of it here."

"But, Johnny, you've lost a lot of time on my account already. Maybe you'd better be trying to make some of it up."

"Speck bein' like he is, we can't move very fast anyway."

"But you wouldn't have me on your hands."

"I don't like the looks of this feller."

"Neither do I. But if he'll take me to San Angelo, that's the main thing. I'll be all right. Don't worry about me."

"I don't like it. Don't like it atall."

"What choice do you have? You'd better go, Johnny. I think if he could get his hands on a gun, he might try to hold you."

Johnny nodded. "Been thinkin' the same thing myself." He looked down, then brought his gaze back up to her face. "Tessie, I like you. I wish we could have met some other way."

"So do I, Johnny. Maybe someday . . ."

He shook his head. "There won't be any someday. We're not comin' back, me and Speck. We can't."

She leaned over. To his surprise, she kissed him on the cheek. He felt his face warm again. "Then good-bye, Johnny. I won't forget you."

Confused, he pulled away abruptly. He reined up beside the paunchy man. "I never did get your name."

"Gerson. Gerson's my name. What's yours?"

Johnny decided to pass the question. "Gerson, you better be sure you take good care of this girl." He looked back at Speck. "Come on, Speck, we got to be movin'."

Riding away, he paused several times to look back. The first time the girl still sat in the wagon, watching them. The next time she was standing in the shade of the arbor, but she was still watching. The third time, just before they rode out of sight, Johnny saw the man standing beside her.

Johnny turned in the saddle, doubt tugging at him.

He and Speck rode half an hour in silence. Speck was slumped forward, fever riding him. Johnny reined up suddenly. "Speck, we oughtn't to've left her there."

Speck made no reply.

"We don't know that Gerson. Did you notice how he looked at her?"

Speck said hoarsely, "Like a coyote lookin' at a cottontail rabbit."

"I'm goin' back for her, Speck."

Speck only shrugged.

Johnny looked about for some shade, though the day was wearing well along toward sundown, and it was no longer particularly hot. He rode to a big mesquite, took his blanket and spread it out beneath the tree. "Lie down there and rest, Speck. I'll be back directly with Tessie and the wagon."

Speck didn't argue. He almost fell out of the saddle. Johnny hurried to help him. When he had Speck set, he swung back onto the brown horse. "Come on, Traveler, let's travel."

Moving in an easy lope much of the way, it took him somewhat less than half an hour to get back. He saw the wagon beside the brush arbor, the team standing droopheaded, not yet unhitched. The man and the girl must be in the house. Johnny wrapped the reins around a post and stepped up to the open door. He heard Gerson's voice.

"Now, girl, you got nothin' to be afraid of."

Gerson hadn't heard Johnny. The man had Tessie backed into a corner, his big left arm braced against the wall to keep her from stepping aside. His right hand was under her chin, and her eyes were wide with fear.

"Get away from her, Gerson!"

The girl cried out in relief. "Johnny!"

Startled, Gerson turned. Instantly the girl darted beyond his reach. She ran across the small room and threw herself against Johnny. "Oh, Johnny, you came back!"

Johnny's fists were clenched. "What have you done to her?"

Gerson shook his head. "Ain't done nothin'."

Tessie Barnett showed her fright. "He told me he was going to the law and tell them about you, unless I would stay here with him. He said he wanted me to be his girl."

Johnny said grimly, "You go on outside, Tessie. Wait for me."

Gently he pushed her aside. But she stayed where she was. "Johnny, he's too big for you. Don't fight him. Let's just go."

"We'll go in a few minutes." Fists tight, he started across the room toward Gerson.

He had been so angry he hadn't thought about Gerson having a gun. But there it was, a rifle propped against a table. Gerson took one quick step and reached it. He brought it up before Johnny could move against him. A wicked smile split Gerson's bearded face. "Just keep on a-comin', cowboy. I'll blow a hole in you as big as your hat!"

Johnny stopped, his mouth dry. He looked down the bore of the rifle at the finger tightening on the trigger. His heart raced. He felt the same helpless fear that had come over him when the cow trader Larramore had brought that pistol up out of his bag.

Behind him, Tessie gave a frightened little cry.

Gerson said, "All I got to do is pull this trigger. You're on the dodge anyway. Likely they'll give me a *re*-ward."

Johnny's heart seemed to be sitting high up in his throat, pounding so hard he would have thought everybody could hear it.

Tessie pleaded, "Don't kill him! I'll do anything!"

Gerson said, "Kind of fancies you, don't she, cowboy? Maybe I ought to take her up on that. Maybe I ought to just let you ride away."

Johnny found his voice. "I wouldn't leave without her."

Gerson nodded. "I know. That's why I got to kill you. Minute I turned my back, you'd be here again, lookin' for a way to kill *me*."

"She'll do you no good, Gerson. Sooner or later she'll get away. She'll tell, and they'll come lookin' for you."

"I'll take care of that in due time."

Johnny saw murder in the man's eyes. He thought of Speck. "My partner's outside," he lied. "Shoot me and he won't let you get out of here alive."

Gerson hesitated. "The sick one? What can *he* do?"

"He can shoot."

Gerson licked his lips, worrying. He had evidently not considered Speck. "You say he's outside?"

Johnny nodded, hoping his eyes would not give away the lie. He had never felt less sure of himself.

Gerson said, "All right, we better go out and talk to him. If he sees I got you-all covered with this rifle, he'll come along easy enough." He motioned toward the girl. "You first. Ease on out that door."

White-faced, Tessie turned toward the opening. Johnny moved carefully along behind her. A dozen ideas raced through his brain, and he dismissed them all. Any sudden action might cause Gerson to kill him by reflex.

Tessie stepped through the door and down to the ground. Johnny paused in the doorway. Tensely, he said, "Tessie, move to one side."

Gerson grunted, "What's goin' on?" But Johnny stood blocking the door. The girl was instantly out of Gerson's sight.

Johnny looked off to his right and spoke loudly as if to Speck. "He's got a gun at my back. If he shoots me, kill him. He can't get out of this house without you gettin' a clear shot at him."

Johnny waited a moment, trying to work up his courage. He sensed Gerson's indecision. Even with a prisoner in his hands, the man had lost his advantage— or thought he had. Johnny got a grip on himself. "If you shoot me now, Gerson, you're as good as dead. This shack of yours will be your coffin. Now, why don't you put that gun down?"

Gerson muttered, "I don't think there's anybody out there."

"Want to stick your head out and look?"

Gerson swallowed. His hand was first tightening, then loosening on the rifle. Johnny's heart was high in his throat. He had never been a poker player because he never could carry off a bluff. He couldn't understand why Gerson didn't see through him. It came to him gradually that Gerson was as frightened as Johnny was.

Again Johnny managed, "The gun, Gerson."

Sweat popped on Gerson's face. His lips quivered. Finally, whipped, he lowered the barrel. "Tell your friend out there I'm puttin' it down."

"Hand it to me," Johnny said, and Gerson did. Johnny took it. "Tessie, come get this."

Tessie came quickly from around the corner. She took the rifle from Johnny's hand as he passed it through the door.

Johnny turned again and looked at Gerson. The fear began draining out of him, and his anger came in a rush. Before Gerson knew what was happening, Johnny was plowing into him, fists swinging.

Normally, with his extra weight, Gerson would have made short work of Johnny Fristo. But Johnny caught him by surprise. The first blow struck Gerson in the stomach. Half the breath gusted out of him, and he staggered. By the time he got his wits together, Johnny had struck him again in the stomach and once across the face.

With a roar of anger Gerson pushed forward. But surprise had cost him too much. From the first blow, Johnny had the advantage. He pressed hard, punching, slashing, driving Gerson back again to the wall. A cold fury welled up and took over for Johnny. He was only dimly aware of the pain when Gerson occasionally managed to strike him.

Gerson fought a losing battle, and he began trying to find a way out. But each time Gerson turned, Johnny was there, striking him again, turning him back. Gerson sank to his knees, his arms raised defensively over his bleeding face.

Reason slowly returned to Johnny. He backed away, breathing hard. He looked down and found his knuckles bruised and bleeding. Each breath he drew hurt him. He paused a moment, looking.

With a sudden lunge he swung one more hard punch into Gerson's face. Gerson fell over and lay on his back.

Gasping, Johnny said, "Now, Gerson . . . don't you ever . . . point a gun at a man again . . . or take advantage of a girl." He backed to the door. "Tessie, the rifle."

Hesitantly she handed it to him. "Johnny, you're not going to kill him . . ."

He shook his head. "I ought to. I would if he made a move. Get to your wagon now, and let's be movin'."

He stayed with the rifle on Gerson till he heard the wagon move. Then he backed out the door and swung into his saddle, the rifle still in his hands. He wondered what Gerson's reaction would be when he came to the door and saw only the two of them riding away.

Johnny went by the corral and chased away a horse he found penned there. That would leave Gerson afoot. With the creek running, there would be no need for horses to come in for water, where Gerson could make an easy catch.

Johnny pulled in behind the wagon and trailed it at some distance. He rode slantways in the saddle, looking back at Gerson's house, the rifle in his hands. For all he knew Gerson might have another rifle somewhere. Johnny didn't want to be caught with his back showing. He rode like that, watching behind him, till he passed over the hill and out of sight of the house. Only then did he relax a little and look ahead of him at the wagon.

It had stopped. Tessie Barnett sat with her hands over her face. As Johnny rode up anxiously, she lowered her hands a little. They were shaking. Her face was milk-white.

"Tessie, what's the matter?"

She motioned for him to sit on the wagon seat beside her. He tied the horse on behind, eased Gerson's rifle down in the wagonbed and climbed up. To his surprise she opened her arms and pulled herself tight against him, burying her face against his chest. Hesitantly he placed his hands on her shoulders and found them trembling.

"Tessie, it's all right now. It's done."

She nodded, but she held him tightly. Her warm body pressed against him, and the effect was like strong whisky. He felt the warm rush of blood to his face.

"Johnny," she said, holding him as if she feared it would kill her to let him go, "I'm sorry to be like this. I don't know what you must think of me."

"I don't think anything bad of you, Tessie, you know that. You've had a couple of hard days."

"I wish I weren't such a baby."

"You're no baby. I don't expect any girl would have done better, and most of them not half as good."

"I won't break down this way again, Johnny. From now on I'll be strong."

"The worst has already happened. Not likely anything as bad will ever happen to you again."

Her arms were still tight around him. She raised her head a little, and he laid his cheek against her forehead. She said, "Somewhere, though, you're going to have to leave me and be on your way, Johnny Fristo. It's going to be hard for me to say goodbye."

He nodded soberly. "How come it had to be like this, Tessie? How come I didn't meet you a few days ago, when I had nothin' to run from, nothin' to be afraid of?"

"I don't know, Johnny. Maybe we just weren't meant to have any luck."

IX

For a long moment a rider sat outlined on the bald top of a rock-strewn hill to the west. Johnny Fristo felt a reflex of fear that stopped his breath and stiffened his hands on the leather lines. Then reason told him this couldn't be Haggard, and he eased. The rider wasn't tall. His shoulders were hunched a little, and his manner of riding showed he wasn't a young man.

He came down through big green clumps of *sacahuista* and reined toward the wagon, taking his time. He rode with the slack ease of a man who had done it all his life, and a long life at that. Gray hair showed beneath an old hat most people would have thrown away a long time ago. He had a salt-and-pepper moustache and tight-drawn skin that looked like saddle leather. His hand lifted in friendly greeting as he approached. Frontier times were fading into the past, but even yet it didn't hurt to let folks know you came in peace.

"Howdy." His voice was pleasant. "You-all lost?" His gaze swept them, and Johnny got the feeling that in two seconds he saw about all there was to see. But looking at the sun-squinted blue eyes, Johnny couldn't tell for the life of him what the man was thinking.

"We're lookin' for a ranchhouse."

"Mine's a little ways over the hill. Would it do?"

"I expect. We got a sick feller here."

The elderly rider eased in closer, stopping his sorrel horse beside the wagon and looking down at the feverish Speck. "You sure do. You oughtn't to be haulin' him around."

"It isn't because we want to."

"Well, we'll take him on up to the house. Sarah'll be so glad to see company, she won't care whether they're sick or well—just so they come."

Tessie Barnett took cheer. "Sarah?"

"My wife. She's the best in the country when it comes to takin' care of the ailin'."

Tessie said thankfully, "We've found a place with a woman."

The rancher studied the girl. "You come a ways, I guess. Bet you're young married folks, headin' west to find a home."

Johnny saw the flush in Tessie's cheeks. "No, sir, we're not married. We just come across this girl a couple of days ago, down the river. She was a-needin' help."

The old rider couldn't hide his curiosity, but he didn't pry. He shoved his hand at Johnny. "My name's Dugan Whitaker."

"Fristo. Johnny Fristo. And this here is Tessie. Back yonder is Speck."

Whitaker's face furrowed. "Fristo! That's got a familiar ring to it. I used to cowboy with a feller by that name back yonder on the San Saba River. Lord, it's been twenty-five or thirty years ago. Baker, his first name was . . . Baker Fristo."

"My dad."

A grin broke across the rancher's wrinkled face. "By George, I ought to've guessed when I looked at you. But it was so long ago the Twin Mountains was just a pair of anthills. You're him all over again. Only, I'll bet you can't ride broncs the way he could."

Johnny wasn't in a smiling mood, but he smiled

now. After Gerson yesterday, it was a relief to come across the kind of people Johnny was used to. "No, sir, I reckon he can still ride rings around me."

Whitaker chuckled. "I expect you do well enough. Bein' Baker Fristo's son, you've had a good raisin'. Come on, let's go to the house."

He let the wagon have the dim trail, and he rode his horse alongside. He talked all the way in. It appeared to Johnny that Whitaker was as thankful for company as his wife could ever be.

"We got a settlement now, a ways yonder over the hills on the upper reach of the Middle Concho. But Sarah, she don't take well to travelin' anymore, so we don't often go, and we don't see many folks." He watched Johnny a great deal, plainly pleased at seeing him. "Sarah knew your dad. She'll be real interested in seein' the kind of man Baker Fristo's son turned out to be."

Johnny chewed his lip. In a way it was good luck, happening into old friends of the family. In a way it wasn't. He dreaded having to explain to them the trouble he was in, he and Speck. With strangers it didn't make so much difference. Here, it would hurt.

Whitaker was talking to Tessie. "We have a daughter not much older than you. She up and married, though, and moved west. These ranches can get awful lonesome for a woman alone. Sarah'll be real tickled to see you."

Johnny brooded awhile. "Mister Whitaker, we got a favor to ask. For Tessie, that is." He explained how he and Speck had come across the girl and her dying father. The old ranchman nodded in sympathy. Johnny said, "We didn't want to just leave her there. We been lookin' for a ranchhouse, somebody to take her to San Angelo."

"And my place is the first one you found?"

Johnny frowned. "Not exactly. We came across one yesterday. Feller named Gerson."

Whitaker cut a quick glance at the girl. "You didn't leave her there with him . . ."

"Not long."

"Pity this country is gettin' so all-fired civilized. Ten years ago they'd have left the likes of Gerson danglin' off of some liveoak tree. He's been awful careless where he puts his brandin' irons."

Johnny said, "He got kind of careless yesterday."

Whitaker glanced again at the girl and read his own meaning. His mouth went grim. "There's other ways than hangin' a man. One day I'll have a talk with some of the boys."

They came in sight of a big growth of china trees, a pair of windmills and a water-filled surface tank that had been hollowed out of the ground by horse, mule and man sweat. Dugan Whitaker had a small rock house built of material hauled down a wagonload at a time from the hills. Johnny flinched, thinking about the untold hours of toil Whitaker must have put in building this place. Yet he knew the pride the old man would have in it, too, for the things a man builds with his own hands are dear to him. They are a part of him, like the hands themselves.

"Sarah," Whitaker called, "we got company."

Johnny expected to see a woman walk out onto the porch, but none did. He thought he glimpsed a face inside, back in the shadows. He couldn't be sure. He knew a moment of doubt. If he *had* seen a woman, there was something odd here.

Whitaker swung down and wrapped one of his

leather reins around a post to hold his horse. He turned toward the wagon. "Let's you and me get ahold of your friend here and carry him into the house."

They lifted Speck carefully. He had enough strength to help a little. They got their arms around him and his over their shoulders. Johnny expected to see the woman come out and hold the screen door open. She didn't. Tessie ran ahead and opened it.

Whitaker took the lead. "Right on back thisaway. We'll put him in the lean-to."

Inside, Johnny caught a glimpse of a woman seated in a chair. Only a glimpse, but it was enough to anger him a little. What kind of hospitality was this, anyway? The least she could have done was to come over and see what the trouble was. He helped Whitaker put Speck on the bed.

"Sarah," said Whitaker, "we got a sick cowboy on our hands."

The woman's voice came from right behind Johnny, and it startled him. He hadn't heard her walk up. He turned and saw her still seated, but the chair was close now. It was a chair with wheels.

"What ails him, son?" she asked Johnny. Johnny was so surprised he couldn't find his voice. The woman smiled gently. "Don't worry, this chair doesn't bother me much anymore. Not like it seems to be botherin' you."

Johnny took off his hat. "I'm sorry, ma'am. I didn't go to stare at you."

"I'll bet you're not a very good poker player. Your eyes give away what's in your head." Her smile widened, and she wheeled the chair in closer to the bed. She repeated, "What's the trouble with your friend?"

Johnny told her. She touched her hand to Speck's head. "Got fever, all right. How's his breathin' been?"

"Short, kind of. He's been in some pain."

She nodded. "I expect he's knockin' at the door of pneumonia. But he may not have crossed over the line yet. Maybe we can hold him back. First thing, you and Dugan get the clothes off of him." She wheeled the chair around and faced Tessie. "Young lady, you want to help? You can reach up into a top shelf in the kitchen and get me some whisky. I'll show you where it's at." She wheeled the chair out about as fast as Tessie could walk.

After the men had removed Speck's clothing and covered him with a blanket, Sarah Whitaker came wheeling back. Tessie brought a steaming cup.

"Now, young fellow," the ranchwoman spoke gently to Speck, "I want you to raise up and drink this. Take it slow, but drink it all." She took the cup from Tessie's hands and passed it over to Speck, keeping a hold on it so he couldn't spill it. Speck swallowed. His flushed face twisted, and for a moment he was about to spit out what she had given him. "Drink it," she said again. Slowly Speck did. The sweat was already popping out on his face.

Mrs. Whitaker said, "That's more whisky than anything else. It'll help boil the fever out of you. Now, girl, if you'll pull up the covers on him, we want to have him sweat the fever out."

Soon Speck was complaining about the heat, and perspiration was rolling from his face. When he made a weak move to push away the covers, Sarah Whitaker firmly pulled them back into place. "It's just something you'll have to go through. Later you'll feel better for it."

After a while Johnny walked out onto the front porch. Now that he had time to look around, he saw things he had missed at first. He saw a slanting ramp by which the wheelchair could roll with comparative ease off and onto the porch. Inside, he had seen how the plank kitchen cabinet had been lowered so everything would be in reach for Sarah Whitaker.

Dugan Whitaker came out onto the shaded porch after him and paused to roll a cigarette. He offered the tobacco sack to Johnny.

Johnny said, "I don't guess it's easy for Mrs. Whitaker, the way she has to get around."

Dugan shook his gray head and licked the edge of the paper. "But she does all right. It was better when our daughter was still livin' here. She was a world of help. You can't keep a girl around forever, though. When they grow up, they got a right to a life of their own. You got to let the fledglings leave the nest."

Johnny fumbled in his shirt pocket for a match. "I don't mean to ask questions that ain't none of my business, but how did it happen? Mrs. Whitaker, I mean?"

"Runaway horse and a buckboard. Had a young horse, not broke long. He boogered at a jackrabbit and commenced to run. Flipped the buckboard over on Sarah out yonder a ways." He pointed. "There where you see that whiteface bull a-grazin'. She crawled all the way to the house for help. Last step she ever took was when she walked out to that buckboard. It's the last step she'll *ever* take."

"Real bad luck."

"Don't waste time feelin' sorry for her. *She* doesn't. Everybody's got a cross of one kind or another to carry. Sarah took the one that was marked for her and made the best of what she had left. She said if it was the devil's work to cripple her, she wasn't goin' to give him the pleasure of seein' her miserable. I guess a strong spirit is worth more than strong legs." He drew thoughtfully on his cigarette. "We all got some-thin' to carry, some trouble that hangs over our heads. Even as young as *you* are, I expect life hasn't been all honey and sweetmilk."

Johnny found the cigarette had lost its taste. He wondered if Whitaker was subtly fishing. Face cloud-ing, he flipped the cigarette out into the clean-swept yard. "Mister Whitaker, before you do anything more for me and Speck, I better tell you about us. You may not want to keep us around."

Whitaker didn't look up. "You fellers are in some kind of trouble, ain't you? I sensed it from the first."

"Then why did you bring us in?"

The ranchman shrugged. "Always did consider myself a pretty good judge of men. I had a good feelin' about you, even before I found out you was Baker Fristo's son. You couldn't have done anything very bad."

Johnny told him about their trouble on the Sonora-San Angelo road, and about Milam Haggard. Listen-ing, Whitaker turned grave.

"Boy, you know Haggard's reputation?"

"I'm afraid I do."

Dugan Whitaker's face was long and sad. He held what was left of the cigarette between his fingers and stared absently at the smoke curling upward from it. He held it so long that the tiny fire went out, and the cigarette turned cold in his fingers. "Goin' to be sev-eral days before your partner is in shape to ride. You got that much time?"

"I don't know. Might have, if the rain wiped out our tracks down on the river. Haggard might be several days pickin' up the trail we left after we got away from the Middle Concho."

"He might, and again he might not. They say he's

got a sixth sense about him." He glanced up in apology. "I didn't mean to talk like that. You know your trouble well enough without me harpin' on it."

"I know the problem all right. I just don't know the answer."

"Seems to me it was your partner that got you into this scrape. You might be able to save yourself if you'd go off and leave him here."

Johnny shook his head violently. "I wouldn't do that."

Whitaker nodded. "I didn't think you would. No son of Baker Fristo ever *could*."

If he was often harsh and demanding of others, Milam Haggard expected no less than perfection in himself. Now that he had found the trail again, he was angry, and the anger was vented in his own direction. Another man might have cursed his quarry or blamed bad luck for the five days he had wasted. Haggard had never been prone to this kind of luxury. In his view the blame was his own, and that was where he placed it.

To be sure, rain had been the main factor. It had wiped out the tracks. But Haggard did not blame the rain. He told himself he should have been more watchful. Upon finding the tracks washed away, he had pondered awhile, then gone forward on the assumption that the fugitives would continue straight up-river. But he had gone all the way west to the head of the Middle Concho and beyond that almost to the Pecos without ever finding a trace. Surely, he had thought, he would have to cut their sign somewhere.

He was certain he knew one cause for his mistake. Those months of trying to become a ranchman—of turning his back on the service of the law—had rusted him a little. But the old training and the hard-learned ability were coming back to him now. It would take something more than two cowboys to throw him again.

Backtracking, working north of the river, he had come across the trail firmly set in the dried mud. For a minute or two the wagon tracks had fooled him, for he had no reason to associate the trail of a wagon with the men he was after. But after some study he had become convinced Fristo and Quitman *were* riding along with a wagon now. Only they and God knew what for. Something else bothered him, too. Several days ago, at about the time he lost the tracks, he had ridden upon a new grave and its headmarker, the endgate out of a wagon. He had worried briefly over the possibility that the cowboys had come across someone and killed him. But considering it, he had told himself it didn't make sense for them to kill a man, then bury him and mark the grave. Hide the body, yes, but not mark the place for all to see. He had decided there was no connection.

Now, finding that the two had been traveling with a wagon, he remembered the grave and wondered again. It seemed foolish for two men under pursuit to encumber themselves with a slow-moving wagon. Unless, of course, there was something of value in the wagon that they didn't want to ride off and leave. That could even provide a motive for killing.

There was still another thing hard to fit into the equation: a woman's shoe prints. A woman was traveling with this wagon; he had no doubt of that.

He had trailed a lot of fugitives in his time. None had ever been harder to figure.

Restless now and angry at himself for the wasted days, he resolved that this would be only a setback, not a defeat. Milam Haggard knew he had time.

Time, in this sort of case, was usually in the favor of the hunter, provided he faced no deadline at which he must turn back. Haggard had no deadline. He was a free agent, responsible only to himself and to God. He could follow these cowboys from now till next year, from here to Hell's front door.

And he would, if he had to.

Riding along watching the trail, he began— without intending to—wondering about himself. He had never been much given to analyzing his own motives. He had always thought in straight and simple lines. There had never been anything devious about Milam Haggard. He had always set a firm course, and everyone who knew him could predict just where he would stand. He had stood for the right and opposed the wrong, and he had not compromised, ever.

Yet now he wondered. Amid the grief for his wife—and, yes, there *was* grief—he found himself taking some sort of grim satisfaction out of this search, almost an enjoyment. He knew this shouldn't be, and it concerned him. It was as if he had somehow been out of his element awhile and on this trail had returned to it.

He told himself this was *not* his true element. He had always told himself he took no pleasure in the hunting of men. He had never killed a man except when he had to, and he had always hated it.

But now he was on a trail again, and in all honesty he would admit to himself that he felt a satisfaction he knew shouldn't be there.

He shook his head. What *was* this, anyway? The whole notion was foolish. He had been well rid of the Ranger job. It was a job for a coyote, not for a man, riding a-horseback from daylight to dark through more long days than he could count, facing furnace

heat in the summer and bitter cold in the winter, all
the time trying to watch the ground for tracks while
his vigilant gaze searched ahead of him. Though he
would never have told anyone, there had always been
a chill playing up and down his back whenever he
rode into a place where someone might lie in wait for
him. Every time he trailed a man, that secret fear
rode with him. Haggard was cold and methodical
when he stood against a man face-to-face. When he
could see his enemy, fear was alien to him.

But always there had been that dread of being shot
from ambush without a chance. The longer he had
ridden with the badge pinned to his vest, the darker
the dread had become. The luckier he was, the more
certain he became that someday his luck would run
out. No gambler could win forever. That was what
Haggard had been—a gambler—betting his life that
he was just a shade better than the other man.

He had grown sick of it, and the dread of ambush
had become a cancerous thing, gnawing at him day
and night. He had been glad when Cora had insisted
that he turn in his badge before they were married. It
gave him a reason to do what he had wanted to do a
long time before.

Yes, sir, he had been well rid of that job. Cora had
been the best thing that ever happened to him.

Now she was dead, and he was at it again, following a dim trail that inevitably led to the death of two
men. It was a miserable thing, and he knew it. Why,
then, this half-ashamed satisfaction?

The saddlegun lay across his lap as he rode down toward Gerson's frame house. Warm dry winds out of
the north and west had almost obliterated the tracks

now, but enough trace was left for Haggard to follow. He saw a man sitting beneath a brush arbor, shading himself from the morning sun. It was a time of day when most men would be out working. Haggard wondered whether this one was sick, lame, or lazy.

The paunchy man stood up at sight of Haggard. People had always said they could tell Haggard was a lawman almost as far as they could see him. There was something about the way he carried himself.

Riding up, Haggard could see a little of both awe and fear in the man's red-veined eyes. Awe and fear were often companions, and hatred usually was not far away.

The man spoke first. "Gerson's my name. Law, ain't you?"

"I'm Milam Haggard." Haggard made no move to shake hands. He found that he disliked this man on sight. He didn't know why; he just had an instinct that way.

"Haggard? I've heard of you. I bet you're huntin' them two cowboys that come through here the other day. I didn't help them none, didn't even give them nothin' to eat. I knowed the law was after them, knowed it the minute they come a-ridin' up here."

"How many days ago?"

The man counted on his fingers. "Five, it was. Maybe six. They're bad ones."

Haggard frowned, his sharp eyes catching the healing remnant of a cut on the man's cheekbone. Fist cut, most likely. "They've got a wagon with them, and a woman, haven't they?"

Gerson nodded eagerly. "They do. I knowed there was somethin' the matter the minute they come in sight. . . ."

Impatiently Haggard broke in. "How about the woman?"

"They had some kind of a story about how her pa had died back down the trail, and how they brought her along to protect her. But if you ask me, they killed him. And they got that girl with them against her will. I tried to take her away from them, but they beat me up. Took both of them to do it, but they beat me up."

Haggard frowned. "How come you didn't go to the law?"

Gerson was hesitant in answering. "I figured the law would be a-comin' here soon enough."

Haggard clenched his fist. "Five . . . six days. It's a lot to make up."

"You can do it. That wagon's slow. And one of the cowboys is sick."

Sick. That made a difference. Haggard wondered how the sick one had been much help in beating up Gerson, but he didn't ask. He figured Gerson had exaggerated that part of the story to make himself look good. Chances were, if Haggard looked, he could find Gerson's description on a "wanted" flyer somewhere.

Gerson said, "One other thing, Haggard. When they left here, they took my rifle."

Rifle! Haggard's mouth went hard. No doubt about it, they meant business now. A woman with them, probably against her will. And a rifle.

It all meant one thing: when he found them, he would have to shoot fast and shoot straight!

X

They had spent almost a week at the Whitaker ranch, and now Speck seemed strong enough to try a hard ride.

In the rosy glow that came before the sunrise, Johnny Fristo tightened his cinch and looked across his horse at Speck swinging a saddle up onto the long-legged bay which Baker Fristo had given him. "Speck, you real sure you can make it now?"

Speck reached under the bay's belly for the saddle girth. "To get away from Milam Haggard, I could ride to Timbuktu."

"You still look a little peaked to me."

"Rather be sick than dead."

Johnny looked back toward the house and saw smoke curling up from the chimney. Out on the other side of the barn Dugan Whitaker was milking a Jersey cow. Johnny could hear the rhythmic strike of milk against the tin bucket as Whitaker squeezed with first one hand, then the other. Up on a shelf over Whitaker's head would be a steaming cup of coffee. Whitaker customarily carried a cup with him when he left the house. Wherever he finished the coffee, he would leave the cup. About once a week he would use up all the cups he had, and he would have to search the barns and corrals, making a roundup. Johnny had helped him with one yesterday.

Johnny said, "Time we get over to the house, they ought to have breakfast ready. Then we'll pull out."

"Let's eat and get started. I can almost smell old

Haggard's breath on the back of my neck. Why he's not already here I'll never know."

A gate opened. Whitaker let his Jersey cow amble slowly out into the pasture. He shut the gate before her calf could get out with her. Whitaker came then, the bucket three-quarters full of milk and foam. He hadn't brought back his coffee cup, but Johnny didn't remind him of it. He figured a man was entitled to at least one bad habit, and this was the only one he had noticed in Whitaker.

The ranchman said, "Well, boys, this'll be your last woman-cooked meal for a while. Let's go get it." He was smiling, but Johnny thought the smile was strained. Whitaker hated seeing them leave, just as Johnny hated having to.

Except for worrying about Haggard, this had been a pleasant week for Johnny. He had spent his time working around the place, patching corrals, bracing a barn, pulling the windmill suckerrods, and changing leathers. He had felt guilty sometimes about not riding out with Whitaker to work cattle. But he hadn't wanted Speck to remain here alone and helpless if Haggard came. Though, if Haggard *had* come, Johnny had no idea what he could have done. One thing sure, Johnny didn't intend to fight him.

He had enjoyed the Whitakers. Dugan Whitaker had been a man much like Johnny's own father. Sarah Whitaker had amazed him constantly with her cheerful way and her uncanny ability to get around and do what she wanted in that wheelchair. He thought Whitaker must have had trouble keeping up with her when she had the use of her legs.

Most of all, Johnny had enjoyed being with Tessie Barnett. The hardest part of leaving was going to be in saying goodbye to her. He didn't know just when he had fallen in love with her, and it didn't really matter. What counted was that he had done it without wanting to, knowing there was no future for them, hoping for her sake that she didn't feel the same way but somehow wishing for his own sake that she did.

Tessie and Sarah Whitaker had breakfast on the table and waiting for them—eggs, steak, gravy, biscuits, coffee. Sarah Whitaker smiled just as Dugan had, and it was easy to see she had to work at it. "Eat aplenty, now. There's a lot of hungry country to the west of here."

Johnny glanced at Tessie. As his gaze touched her, she turned half around, hiding her face from him.

Dugan Whitaker set his bucket of milk on the cabinet for straining. "I don't want to seem like I'm pushin' you fellers, but it's gettin' daylight outside. I think for your sakes you better eat and get a move on."

Johnny had noted at least one sign of renewed strength in Speck: appetite. All his life Speck had made a good hand at the table or around the chuck wagon. As for Johnny, he felt a wintry sadness about leaving, and he had to push to make himself eat.

Mrs. Whitaker said, "Tessie and me, we've made an agreement, Johnny. She's not goin' to San Angelo."

Johnny looked up sharply.

Tessie said, "They've asked me to stay here with them, Johnny."

"That's right," Sarah put in. "She's got no place particular to go anyway. All she could earn in San Angelo would be a livin'. She'll get that here. She's been a world of help and company to us, like our daughter used to be."

Tessie nodded, and her eyes glistened a little. "That way, Johnny, you'll know where I am."

Johnny had worried about how she would fare in San Angelo. "That's fine, Tessie." He finished eating before Speck did. He said, "Speck, I'll go bring up the horses while you finish."

He walked out to the barn, taking his time, looking around him slowly. He wanted to remember this place. In time to come it might be a refuge for him—in his mind—a place for a restful mental retreat when the world seemed to close in around him. He glanced up at one of Whitaker's coffee cups balanced on a low rafter beneath a shed, and he smiled.

He had taken several minutes before he led the horses out the gate and closed it behind him. He swung up on Traveler, leading Speck's bay. A movement at the house caught his eye. He jerked his head around and saw Tessie running toward him, skirts flaring. "Hurry, Johnny, hurry!"

She pointed, and he saw the horseman outlined atop the hill, the sun rising like a golden ball of fire behind him.

Johnny didn't need binoculars. One glance and he somehow knew with a dreadful certainty. This was Milam Haggard!

The horses, fresh and rested, spooked backward as the girl rushed toward them. "Run, Johnny! You've still got time. Run!"

For a moment Johnny sat there confused and undecided, his hands tight on the reins. What good would it do now to run? Haggard would catch them. Yet, if they stayed and waited, what could they do?

"I'll get Speck," he said, and touched spurs to Traveler's ribs. He moved into a long trot, leading the bay toward the house.

"Speck! Come a-runnin'!"

But Speck didn't come. Johnny reined up at the

house and shouted again. Sarah Whitaker pushed the screen door open with her chair and wheeled out onto the porch. "Johnny, he's taken the rifle and gone out the back."

"The rifle?"

For the first time in days Johnny remembered the rifle he had wrestled from Gerson. Except for this, they would have ridden off and forgotten it.

Dropping the bay's reins, he pulled his horse about and spurred around the house. "Speck! Speck, come back here!"

He glanced again toward Haggard. The ex-Ranger was quartering across toward the ranch headquarters, his dun horse in a steady trot. A pack horse followed. Speck was hunkered down behind a cedar. Johnny saw that in a few moments Haggard would ride in front of him. It occurred to Johnny then that Haggard had not seen Speck.

Speck—if he could hold himself in check long enough—could wait where he was and shoot Haggard out of the saddle at almost point-blank range.

For just a moment Johnny knew a sense of relief. That was an out. With Haggard dead they stood a chance.

But he knew this wasn't the way. The death of Haggard's wife had not actually been their fault, but this would put blood on their hands that would never wash away. They might be forgiven for the death of Cora Haggard, but never the murder of this man.

"Speck, hold up! Don't do it!"

Shouting, Johnny spurred into a run. "Speck, for God's sake put it down!"

Haggard saw Johnny moving toward him, and Johnny saw the man's hands come up holding a saddlegun. From behind him he heard Tessie scream.

Speck brought up his rifle and leveled it across a branch of the cedar.

Johnny cried again, "No!"

Speck's rifle spat flame. Haggard rocked back, dropped the saddlegun, slumped forward and spilled out of the saddle. Haggard's horse jumped clear, wild-eyed with fright.

Speck straightened and began running toward Haggard, levering another cartridge into the breech. Johnny saw Haggard try vainly to push up onto his hands and knees.

Haggard still lived, and Speck was going to shoot him again.

Johnny spurred savagely. Speck hadn't listened to him before, and he wouldn't listen now. Speck heard the horse running. He stopped to look behind him, his eyes wide and desperate. Seeing Johnny meant to stop him, he turned and began running, trying to reach Haggard and finish him before Johnny could ride him down.

Speck stopped and raised the rifle to his shoulder. As he brought it level with Haggard's bent body, Johnny reached him. Johnny leaned from the saddle and grabbed at Speck as he rode by. He succeeded only in knocking him down. The rifle roared, the bullet plowing harmlessly into the ground. In desperation Speck scrambled on hands and knees, trying to reach the rifle. Johnny quit the saddle and came running. He got to the rifle just as Speck's fingers closed on the stock of it. He kicked, and the rifle went flying.

Speck turned his face upward, and Johnny saw that his partner was frantic with fear and rage. "Let me kill him, Johnny! Let me kill him!"

Johnny grabbed his friend's arms and tried to hold him. "Speck, come out of it!"

"We got to kill him, Johnny!"

Speck began fighting like a tiger, swinging his fists, kicking wildly. For a fleeting moment Johnny had time to wonder where Speck's strength came from. Then he was too busy fighting back.

"Speck, stop it!"

Speck threw himself at Johnny, punching savagely, shouting incoherently. Murder boiled in Speck's wild eyes.

There was no time now for regrets. Johnny put them aside soberly and fought as if he had never seen Speck before, as if this weren't the best friend he had in the world. He tried to avoid Speck's face with his fists. He punched Speck in the belly and the ribs with all the power he had. Speck had to be stopped.

Speck began losing the sudden desperate strength born of his fear. The fever weakness pulled him down. He slumped to his knees, hugging his arms against his sides, tears streaming down his face.

"Kill him, Johnny! You got to kill him!"

"Speck, haven't we done enough to him already?"

"It's him or us!"

"Then it'll have to be us!" Johnny turned away and reached down for the rifle. He opened the bolt, then smashed the weapon against the trunk of a cedar. He swung it again and again until he knew for sure it was broken and bent beyond any possible use. He pitched it away and stood a moment with pounding heart as he tried to get back his breath.

He walked to Haggard, dreading to look at the man. Haggard was on his knees, hunched over in pain. He wore a pistol, but he had made no move to draw it. He seemed paralyzed. Johnny drew the pistol from its holster and pitched it off into the brush.

"Let me see, Mister Haggard. How bad did he hit you?"

If Haggard heard, he gave no sign of it. His face was flour-white, his thin lips drawn tight against his teeth in a grinding agony. His right hand was gripped against his left shoulder, and blood dribbled between his clawed fingers.

"I'm sorry, Mister Haggard. I swear to God, I'm sorry."

Dugan Whitaker came, half running, half hopping. Tessie came, too, though she halted behind Haggard as if afraid to look at him. Johnny raised his eyes. "Mister Whitaker, we got to get him to the house." He glanced back over his shoulder. "Speck, you done it. Now you come help."

They carried Haggard as far as the porch. Whitaker said, "Tessie, you run in and fetch a blanket out here. That slug's still in him, and I got to have daylight to find it."

They laid Haggard out and tore the shirt off of him. They brought whisky to give him for the pain, but he passed into unconsciousness without needing it. Dugan Whitaker tried probing for the bullet, but his old hands would not hold still.

"Johnny, it's up to you. You can save him, or you can stand back and watch him die. But remember: if you save him, you know one day he'll still come lookin' for you."

Johnny grimly studied Haggard's gray face. "Give me the probe."

He got the bullet out. They washed the wound with whisky, then Sarah Whitaker used handfuls of flour to stop the bleeding. When they could, they carried him into the lean-to. They placed him on the same bed where Speck had lain.

"Mrs. Whitaker," Johnny said apologetically, "you got another one to tend. We don't bring you nothin' but trouble."

"The Lord's wish, not yours."

Johnny watched Speck closely, wondering if he might try again. But the spirit was gone from Speck now. He had made his try and failed. He stood with his shoulders drooped, eyes dulled by hopelessness.

Dugan Whitaker said, "Well, at least you got time now. It'll be a long while before he goes after you again."

Haggard stirred. Consciousness slowly returned to him. He blinked, trying to focus his eyes. Johnny stood beside his bed. "It's me, Mister Haggard. Me, Johnny Fristo. I just want you to know I'm sorry for what happened."

Haggard winced with pain, but he forced himself to hold his eyes a moment on Johnny. And Johnny saw the same implacability he had seen that day on the Sonora road.

Haggard's voice was thin, but it had a fierceness to it. "I won't be here long. One day soon I'll be lookin' for you again. And I vow, boy, I'll find you!"

Johnny turned away sadly, his head down. Why try to tell him again it had been Larramore who had killed his wife? Haggard hadn't believed him before. He would believe him even less now. Johnny dug into his pocket for the money Baker Fristo had given him.

"He'll be needin' a doctor, Mister Whitaker. You get him one, and pay him with this."

"You'll need that money yourself."

Johnny shook his head. "If it hadn't been for us,

he wouldn't be here. Take it, please." He stopped and picked up a sack of food which Tessie and Mrs. Whitaker had prepared. "Come on, Speck. Let's go."

Outside, he tied the sack onto his own saddle, not trusting Speck to do it this time. He said goodbye first to Sarah, then to Dugan Whitaker. Last he took Tessie's hands. "Tessie, it's been awful good to know you. Take care of yourself."

"Johnny . . ." She would have said more, but the words died. She leaned forward and kissed him on the lips, then pulled her hands free and turned her back, her head bowed.

Johnny rode away, looking over his shoulder. Speck followed him like a whipped dog. Johnny kept looking back, seeing the Whitakers watching him, seeing that Tessie had turned once more and was watching him too.

Suddenly Johnny stopped his horse. "Speck, wait here. I'll be back."

He turned Traveler around and spurred into a long trot. He stepped to the ground in front of Tessie. He grabbed her into his arms with such a violence that his hat fell off and hit the ground at his feet.

"Tessie, Tessie, I don't want to leave you."

"And I don't want you to leave. But what can we do?"

"I'll send for you, that's what." He held her at arm's length and looked into her glistening eyes. "Someday, somewhere, I'll come onto a place that's so far out of the way Haggard'll never be able to find it. When I do, and when I get settled, I'll write to you, Tessie. I'll send for you."

"Promise, Johnny?"

"I promise. Now that I've known you, Tessie, I couldn't live without you anymore."

"I'll wait, Johnny, and I'll be ready. I'll follow you if you go ten thousand miles."

He held her again, once, then he turned on his heel, swung up into the saddle and rode away.

Inside the house, Milam Haggard's teeth were clenched against a searing pain. But the pain did not keep him from hearing.

XI

They quartered west by southwest, skirting the upper reaches of Centralia Draw and pointing in a general way toward ancient Horsehead Crossing. They rode dry all day through greasewood and stunted mesquite and patches of prickly pear. Not even a windmill showed on the skyline. They were west now of any living waters which would feed into the Middle Concho. This was the desolate stretch of lizard and rattlesnake and chaparral-hawk country which had brought misery and desperation to untold numbers of travelers making their way toward the unfriendly river known as the Pecos.

Before night they reached the China Pond. In front of them, and all to the south, stretched a long line of flat blue mountains. Their profile was low, but Johnny knew they were rough, impassable for wagons and difficult for horsemen. All trails led across the desert toward a scalloped opening near the northern edge. This would be Castle Gap, known for centuries as a pointer to Horsehead just beyond.

"This is a good place to stop, Speck. We got water here."

Speck only nodded. He had sulked all day, speaking perhaps half a dozen words since they had left the Whitaker ranch. This was remarkable for Speck. Instead of riding alongside Johnny, he had hung back half a length. When Johnny would slow to allow Speck to pull up even with him, Speck would draw back and keep the distance about the same. His brooding eyes avoided Johnny.

They made camp at the China Pond. Automatically Speck rode off to try to gather up some firewood. He came back without any, and Johnny used dried cowchips for fuel to cook a little supper. Later Speck sat back from the tiny fire and ate listlessly, keeping his own counsel. Johnny watched him, wondering what dark thoughts plodded through Speck's troubled mind.

"Speck, you still mad at me because of this mornin'?"

Speck didn't answer.

"I had to do it. We're not killers."

Speck's gaze touched him a moment. Resentfully he said, "You fought me. You used to call yourself my friend, and you fought me."

"I'm still your friend."

A pent-up anger began boiling over. "No, you ain't. You think you're better than I am. I've felt it comin' on ever since we stopped in Angelo. Aunt Pru told you about me, and my mother. Now I'm not good enough for you anymore. I'm trash."

"Speck, that's the silliest notion I ever heard of."

"No, it isn't. There was a time you wouldn't have fought me for nothin' in this world. Now you'd like to take that girl and ride off and leave me. But you can't because you know we're in this together. You're stuck with me and you hate it. You hate *me*."

Johnny's impatience melted away, for his pity was stronger. "You're all mixed up, Speck. I like you the same as I always did. If it's any consolation to you, what your Aunt Pru said didn't make any difference atall. I've known about your mother for years."

Speck stared incredulously. "You mean you always knew, and you never let on?" Johnny nodded. Speck exploded. "That makes it even worse. All these years you been actin' like my friend, and all the time you was probably snickerin' at me behind my back."

He stood up and stomped off to where he had pitched his blanket to the ground. He spread it out and flopped down on his back, lying there and staring angrily up at the darkening sky.

Johnny's jaw took on a hard set. No use arguing. Speck had a haywire way of thinking, sometimes. He'd come around by and by.

At least, Johnny hoped he would.

Next morning they went on to the gap. Johnny noticed horse and cattle bones all along the way. This had always been a cruel trail. Curiosity held him in the gap awhile. Nearby he found the burned remnants of several wagons. He wondered if these were the result of some long-ago Indian attack, a bandit raid or if someone had just gotten careless with fire. If a raid, there was no question about the outcome. If an accidental fire, what had the victims done afterward? Here, so far from civilization, the loss of wagons and supplies in those earlier times could have meant the same eventual outcome: death. There was no way to know for sure now, for the charred wooden skeletons and the dark ashes had been reduced by long years of probing wind and occasional rain. Johnny sat on his horse and looked, and he let his imagination sweep him away. For a while he wished he could have been born fifty years earlier.

But eventually he heard Speck grumbling about how they ought to be going, and he grudgingly came back to reality, back to his own problems. Trouble, he knew, was something each generation shared.

No one had a monopoly on it.

Johnny pointed across the gently rolling stretch of

greasewood which lay below. "Down yonder, Speck, is Horsehead Crossing. Been a lot of history made along here."

Speck was still grumpy but a little more disposed to talk this morning. "Maybe you can see the history, but all I can see is a lizard-lick of a country that ain't worth a Mexican dollar if you got back ninety cents change."

They followed the bone-strewn trail twelve miles and came at last to the river. Here was fabled Horsehead with its sloping banks which led down to swift-moving water. This was the only place for a long journey up or down the river where the banks were such that wagons and livestock could go down into the water with a reasonable chance of coming out again on the opposite side.

A big scattering of animal bones lay along here. At this spot some thirty years before, Charles Goodnight had lost part of a Longhorn cattle herd in alkaline water and treacherous quicksands, and had pronounced the Pecos River the graveyard of a cowman's hopes.

Johnny saw a trail that angled off upriver. "This ought to lead the way up to the salt lake, Speck. That's where Dugan Whitaker told us to go."

Speck shivered, though the morning was warm. "Let's get ridin', then. This place makes my skin crawl."

They followed the wagon trail northwestward, roughly paralleling the snaking river and its line of salt-cedar trees. As they approached the Juan Cordona salt lake, the hard alkali soil began giving way gradually to more of sand. Heat waves shimmered on the horizon as the salt basin came into view.

They met a Mexican burro train moving downriver,

the plodding little beasts carrying a heavy burden of white salt in huge twin baskets of rawhide and green willow. The ragged Mexican at the head of the train stared briefly at the cowboys, his eyes all but hidden under the wide, floppy brim of an incredibly old sombrero. He nodded, spoke a two-word greeting and walked on. Johnny watched the short-stepping burros move by him, the salt baskets bobbing from side to side with the rhythm of their walk. The Mexican *mulateros* were grayed with dust, their tattered shirts soaked with sweat and clinging to their bodies. Only one wore shoes, and these had been patched with rawhide. The rest had only simple *huaraches,* a thick sole held to the foot by leather thongs, protecting against thorns, sharp rocks and burning sand.

Johnny said solemnly, "Whenever a man gets to feelin' sorry for himself, he needs to take a look at somebody worse off than he is."

Speck grunted. "I bet they ain't got Milam Haggard lookin' for them."

The "lake" was a vast irregular stretch of shining salt, lying in an ancient basin rimmed by sandhills. The level bottom glistened in the sun, though along the edges a thin skim of dust had settled and turned it brown. There was feed here for livestock—a scattering of sand-type bunchgrasses and weeds. There was the tough green beargrass with its rapier-like stems and the tall yucca stalks. And here and there about the lake lay a dotting of camps, salt haulers of all types.

Johnny and Speck rode into two burro camps without finding anyone who spoke English. The third camp they found had half a dozen heavy wagons already full of salt and several more wagons in the process of being loaded by Mexican help. A crew sweated in the sun, their shovels slowly pitching dry salt into the wagons. A dark-skinned man saw the cowboys and came walking toward them. His beard was black beneath a crust of dust and salt. Johnny took him for a Mexican until he spoke. "Howdy. You-all lookin' for somebody in particular?"

Johnny nodded. "We're supposed to find a feller name of Massingill."

The salt freighter stared at the pair, his eyes narrowed. "You-all ain't lawmen or somethin'? Ain't got a warrant for somebody?"

Johnny shook his head. "No, sir, we just got a letter for Mister Massingill, is all. Friend of his sent it. Man name of Dugan Whitaker."

The bearded man smiled. His shoulders sagged in relief. "That's different. My name happens to be Massingill. Folks call me Gyp, on account of the Pecos River water I tote in my barrels." He reached up to shake hands. "Afraid at first you might be star-packers. I'm already shorthanded, and I sure didn't want you takin' off none of my help. You say you got a letter?"

Johnny handed him a letter which Dugan Whitaker had spent an hour in writing by lamplight the night before Johnny and Speck had left the ranch. "We're in kind of a jackpot, Mister Massingill. Dugan Whitaker, he thought you might be able to help us."

Massingill squatted in the shade of a wagon. It took him almost as long to read the letter as it had taken Whitaker to write it. His index finger followed the lines as he slowly read, his lips forming the words. At last he looked up. "A jackpot, you say? Looks to me like it's a right smart worse than that. I've seen Milam Haggard. How far behind you is he?"

Johnny explained about the shooting at the Whitaker ranch.

Massingill frowned suspiciously. "You-all must've known old Dugan a long time."

Johnny shook his head. "Never met him before."

"You sure must've convinced him you was all right. Or maybe you held a gun at his head to make him write this letter."

"No, sir, he wrote it of his own accord. He was awful good to us, him and Mrs. Whitaker both. This is the first time we ever been in trouble. They knew it."

Massingill studied them awhile, his eyes keen. They burned like the sun through a magnifying glass. Finally he nodded. "Well, if you convinced old Dugan, I guess that'll do for me. He's not an easy man fooled." He folded the letter and shoved it into his pocket. "And if Haggard has been laid up with a bullet in him, that means you got some time. We don't have to do things in a hurry. I'll make you a swap. You help me, and I'll help you."

Johnny nodded eagerly. "Anything you want."

"Well, the way I see it, Haggard will be a-lookin' for you-all to go on west. That's where any smart man on the dodge would go. So we'll fool him. Soon's I get these wagons full I'm takin' this salt south, down the Pecos River. There's ranches off down in there that a man wouldn't find in a hundred years if he didn't know where to look. It's a big country, some of it so big and dry that a hawk won't leave the nest without it carries a canteen. I'll take you down there with me, and I'll get you a job on some outfit where the whole United States army couldn't find you."

"That's mighty good of you, Mister Massingill."

"Gyp! And don't thank me till you find out how

good your hands fit a shovel handle. I'll swap you a ride on my wagons in return for your muscles and your sweat. Sooner we get them wagons loaded with salt, the sooner we start down the river.

"You'll find the shovels over yonder!"

XII

Patience was part of a manhunter's stock in trade—difficult to learn, but indispensable. Milam Haggard had learned it long ago. It served him well now in this small settlement on the Centralia, for without it he could not have forced himself to remain here idle—waiting, watching, biding his time. It had been most of three months now since he had lain bleeding at the Whitaker ranch, listening to fading hoofbeats as the two cowboys rode away.

Even without hearing it, he sensed the speculation which his long stay had started among the townspeople and the ranchmen who ranged their cattle on bluestems and tobosa grass up and down the creeks and draws. He had not chosen to tell them why he had remained here, though doubtless they could guess most of it. Only one person in town, besides himself, knew the full reason.

To be sure, the whole country knew who he was and knew of his mission. They knew his wife had died as an innocent bystander in a fight along the Sonora-San Angelo road. They knew Haggard had been shot at the Whitaker ranch and that he had come riding in here as soon as he was able to mount a horse by himself, disclaiming any further help from the cowboys' friends. It was common knowledge that Dugan and Sarah Whitaker would still argue the fugitives' case to anyone who cared to listen.

It was well known also that Haggard was no longer a Ranger, that he had been unable to get official backing in his search for the two cowboys. At least two Ranger friends, to the knowledge of the townspeople, had come here to talk with him. Common belief was that they were trying to talk him out of his quest.

Why then, people asked each other, was he still here? Granted, his left shoulder was still stiff and appeared to give him some pain. But those who from afar had watched this gaunt, unsmiling man at target practice beyond the edge of town could testify that his eye was keen and his aim was ungodly straight. Haggard lived in a small shack on which he paid a token rent. Though civil enough, he made no effort to cultivate new friendships. He received no company except for a couple of ranchmen who had known him down south in the Ranger service. They stopped in occasionally to see how he was getting along, for they felt a genuine concern. He spent his time reading, exercising the shoulder and practicing at targets.

Some careful observers had noted that he always watched the mail hack when it arrived at the small general store that served as a post office. Inevitably he was among the first to be there as the storekeeper sorted the mail. It had become something of a routine, which seldom varied. Haggard would go straight to the corner where the mail was put up in small individual boxes. "Anything today, John?"

The storekeeper would always shake his head. "Maybe next time."

It had become so repetitious that the early flurry of speculation had died down, and many people largely lost interest. Most agreed he was either awaiting a renewal of his Ranger commission to make his search legal, or during his long recovery period he had sent someone ahead to track down the fugitives and now waited for word as to their whereabouts.

Whatever the storekeeper knew, he wasn't talking.

Milam Haggard had never been a drinking man. He did not believe it wise in his trade. Often he had observed how liquor had made quarry fall easy prey to a gun in the hands of a sober man.

But Haggard was a lonelier man than most people suspected, and once in a while he welcomed a visit from old friends. On such occasions, though he did not drink, he sometimes accompanied his friends to the saloon and sat there to enjoy their companionship.

Thus it was that he happened to walk into the place one afternoon and find himself face-to-face with the cattle trader Larramore.

Larramore was playing cards with two prospective cow buyers. The surprise was mutual. Larramore's eyes opened wide and frightened, his face losing color. In Sonora that day after Cora Haggard's death, Larramore had sensed how close he came to being shot when the sheriff told Milam Haggard about the swindle against the two cowboys. Though Haggard blamed the shooting directly on Johnny Fristo and Speck Quitman, he had immediately grasped the fact that Larramore's duplicity had provoked the incident. Haggard's granite fist had sent Larramore reeling. Larramore had lain terrified, not moving, knowing that if Haggard had been wearing a gun he would have killed him without ceremony and without regret.

Seeing Haggard now, Larramore arose shakily, his voice strained. "Haggard, I been tryin' to stay out of your way just like you told me. I had no idea you was here." His glance dropped anxiously to the six-shooter on Haggard's right hip.

Haggard only stared at him, his eyes hard and hating.

Larramore watched Haggard's right hand. "Haggard, I ain't got a gun on me." That was a lie, for he carried a small .38 in his boottop. But he feared if Haggard even suspected its presence, he might force Larramore to reach for it. It would have been no contest.

Haggard's narrowed eyes seemed to crackle with danger. "Larramore, those cowboys still claim you were the one who really fired the shot. I know you said you didn't, but I want to hear you say it again."

Larramore trembled. "It was *them*. They both had guns."

"That's a lie. Only one of them had a gun. And *you* had one."

"It was *them* that killed her. It was them!" The trader dropped his chin, unable to look into Haggard's face.

Haggard cut his gaze to the two men who had been playing cards at the table with Larramore. One he recognized as a rancher south of here. He took the other for a rancher, too. They sat watching in surprise, not quite comprehending. Haggard asked, "You-all have business with this man?"

One of them replied hesitantly, "He told us he knew where there was some cattle we could buy worth the money."

Haggard's voice was raw. "You'd better have nothin' to do with him. He's a thief, a liar and a cheat!"

Larramore jerked his head up. "Haggard, you got no right . . ."

Haggard's eyes cut back to him, and they were deadly. Larramore's words stuck in his throat. Haggard's voice sliced like the razor edge of a skinning knife. "Leave town, Larramore. Leave this part of the country. Next time I see you, I'll probably kill you!"

He turned sharply and started for the door. Larramore stared after him, frozen.

Haggard had just reached the door when the bartender shouted. Instinctively he jumped to one side, whirling as his right hand dropped and came up with the six-shooter.

Larramore crouched awkwardly, having reached down to his boottop for the .38. No gunman, he fired wildly. The bullet smacked into the doorframe and sent wood splinters flying. He never got a chance to fire again. Haggard's pistol roared like thunder inside the small saloon. Larramore stepped back under the driving impact. He began bending forward from the waist, the .38 slipping from his fingers. He screamed. Then the scream died off, and he pitched forward onto his face.

Haggard cautiously moved toward him, kicking the .38 out of the way. He stooped and turned Larramore over into his back, the strain bringing a stabbing pain to the old shoulder wound. "How about it, Larramore? *Was* it you who killed her?"

Larramore made a feeble effort to speak. Then he went limp. He died with his eyes and his mouth open.

Haggard pushed to his feet, the shoulder throbbing a little. He shook his head and spoke to no one in particular. "It doesn't matter, I guess. They *all* killed her."

It was a rare occasion when Dugan Whitaker came to town. Since Milam Haggard had ridden away from the Whitaker ranch on his dun, slumped over the saddle horn in pain but too proud to remain any longer under that roof, he had seen Whitaker only once. They had nodded civilly and gone their separate ways. Taking care of his place virtually alone, Whitaker didn't have much time for coming to the settlement.

But this morning, sitting in front of the shack and watching the dark clouds which built threateningly in the north, Haggard saw the Whitakers pass by in their buckboard. Dugan and Sarah Whitaker gave him a polite nod, but nothing more. The Barnett girl only stared, and Haggard thought he saw fear leap into her face. During the time he had been at the ranch, wounded, the girl had kept her distance as if he had been a rattlesnake.

Haggard regretted that. He saw fear everywhere these days, since he had killed Larramore. He wanted respect, not fear. But that was part of the business. He had come to expect it, even if he didn't welcome it.

He hadn't been back to the saloon. He doubted he would ever go. As he heard it, the bartender hadn't even cleaned up the blood. He had purposely left it to soak a dark stain deep into the wood. Now it had become an attraction for the idle curious. This brought a rush of resentment every time it crossed Haggard's mind. He was not an exhibitionist. Killing a man had never pleased him. He had always dreaded it, and he had regretted it when it was done.

He had thought there might be a grim pleasure in killing someone who had had a part in Cora's death. But to his surprise the sight of Larramore dead on that dirty saloon floor had brought only the same old revulsion to sicken him.

Of late he had spent much time thinking about his ranch up on the Colorado River. He had a few cowboys hired, and he felt sure they were taking care of it for him. But he wished he could go up there, find out how things looked, see if summer rains had greened the grass and fattened the cattle. He had grown to hate his vigil here. The thought of following another long trail in a lonely search for fugitives was abhorrent to him.

But again, there was his training, and his pride. He had made a vow over the fresh mound where they had laid Cora to rest. He had never broken a vow in his life. He wouldn't break this one, though sometimes he had to conjure up a vision of Cora's face to give him the strength that he could carry on this way.

Watching the Whitakers' buckboard wheel on down toward the heart of the settlement, Haggard suddenly remembered this was the day for the mail hack. And it was due about now, give or take an hour. He didn't want the Whitakers receiving their mail before he got there.

Squaring his hat, he started up the dusty road afoot. To his satisfaction he found the Whitaker buckboard sitting in front of a different store. Dugan Whitaker and Tessie Barnett were lifting Sarah Whitaker down into her wheelchair. Haggard looked east on the wagon road that led in from San Angelo. He saw dust. He wondered if that would be the mail hack.

Well, this was going to be cutting things pretty fine. He sat down on an empty bench at the front of the store to wait. His gaze drifted up and down the street, cutting back often to the Whitaker buckboard. He hoped they wouldn't come over this way before the hack got in.

The driver pulled up, the dust drifting on ahead of him. He nodded at Haggard and carried the mail bag inside. Haggard kept his seat awhile, giving the storekeeper time to put up the mail. There wasn't any hurry about it, so long as the Whitakers didn't come. Even so, it seemed it took an awfully long time.

Finally the hack driver came out and nodded again, wiping his mouth. The storekeeper always had coffee ready for him. He took time to drink it before he traveled on. Haggard glanced through the window constantly to see if the mail had been sorted. The seat of his pants prickled with impatience. When he saw the storekeeper leave the mail corner, he arose and walked inside.

The storekeeper's eyes met his, and Haggard knew even before the man nodded. "It came, Mister Haggard."

"You're sure?"

The storekeeper nodded again. "It's addressed to Miss Tessie Barnett, care of Dugan Whitaker."

"Let me have it, John."

"Well, now, I can't be doin' that. It's agin the law."

"Damn the law! Give me that letter!"

"I promised I'd tell you when it came. I didn't tell you I'd give it to you. It's still the U.S. mail, Mister Haggard, till the girl puts her hands on it. There can't nobody touch it. Not you and not me."

Anger swelled in Haggard. He was sorely tempted to walk across and take the letter anyway. But judgment stopped him. Unreasoning anger was another luxury he had never allowed himself. "All right. I'll wait."

He walked to the door and started to go outside. But he saw Tessie Barnett on her way, walking rapidly several steps in front of old Dugan Whitaker. Haggard stepped back, looking quickly around him. He saw an open door leading into a storeroom. "Not a word, John." He stepped through the door and out of sight.

Tessie came in, Dugan Whitaker hurrying along in a vain effort to catch up with her. "Tessie," he laughed, "go easy. Have some pity on an old man."

Tessie might as well not have heard him. Eyes sparkling in anticipation, she searched out the storekeeper. "Do you have any mail for me? Tessie Barnett?"

The storekeeper took his time, glancing at the open storeroom door. He knew what was about to happen. "Yes, ma'am, I believe maybe I do." He walked over to the corner and sought out a letter from among a dozen. Regretfully he placed it in her eager hands. "This what you've been waitin' for?"

Excitement leaped into Tessie's face. "Uncle Dugan, it's from *him*; I *know* it is!"

Haggard stepped out of the storeroom, unnoticed by Tessie and Whitaker. The storekeeper turned his back and walked away, wanting no part of this. Tessie ripped the envelope open, her hands trembling. "Uncle Dugan, it *is* from him, it *is*!"

Milam Haggard stepped up beside her and snatched the letter from her hands. "I'll take that!"

She whirled. Seeing him, she raised one hand up over her mouth. Her eyes were big as dollars. "You!"

Dugan Whitaker made a grab for the letter. "Haggard, you got no right!"

Haggard stepped back and turned half around, keeping the letter out of his reach. "I *have* got the right."

He skipped the opening lines, for they spoke of loneliness, and he knew all there was to know about that. His gaze dropped farther down in the letter:

This is a good ranch. A little on the plain side, maybe, but your going to like it here Tessie. Theres a good adobe house the owner says we can live in. Kind of little but big enough for two. I think we can slip down to Langtry and get Judge Bean to marry us without anybody paying us much notice.

You would never find the place by yourself. So
will meet you at Horsehead Crossing on the Pecos.
Maybe Mr. Whitaker can bring you or get somebody
to. Will be there about Sept. the 15. Bring your
wagon. Will wait till you come and please hurry.

Horsehead Crossing! Haggard crunched the letter
in his hand. September the fifteenth! Why, that was
yesterday! This letter must have traveled halfway
around the world before it reached here.

So Fristo was already there, waiting! And Quitman with him, if Haggard was any judge.

He knew a quiet moment of triumph, then his
face turned grave. A chill passed down his back as
he turned to Tessie Barnett and saw the dismay in
her eyes. It struck him that she was a pretty girl.
Silently he handed her the letter. Sympathy touched
him. Pity she had gotten mixed up in this. Pity she
had to know the heartbreak that was coming. But
she was young, and she would survive. In time she
might even learn to understand the necessity of it.
Anyway, there was no choice. The die had been
cast. Haggard had long since developed an instinct
for the inevitable. The thing was coming to an end
now, as sure as the sun would rise and set tomorrow.

The girl's eyes pleaded. "Mister Haggard, you
can't do it. Please, say you're not going to do it!"

She had as well have talked to the big wood heater
that stood cold and unused in the center of the store.
Haggard looked at Dugan Whitaker. "I'm sorry it's
this way, Mister Whitaker. I think you'd best take her
home." He turned his back and walked to the door.
Tessie stared after him, the letter crushed in her hand.
The dismay had turned to terror.

"No!" she screamed and went running after him.

Haggard hurried his step a little, wanting to get away from her. He went down off the porch and into the dusty street, his eyes set on the barn where his dun horse was kept stabled. Clouds were darkening overhead.

"Mister Haggard, wait!"

He tried to outwalk her. How could a man argue over a thing like this? How could he explain why he had to go on? For God's sake, didn't she already know?

She grabbed his good arm. Head high, he kept walking, his strength pulling her along. "Please, Mister Haggard, listen to me. What good will it do to kill him? Will *she* come back? Will another wrong make things right?" He walked on, trying not to listen. "I love him, Mister Haggard. If you loved *her*, you should understand that."

He swallowed, trying to shut his ears. She stepped in front of him, still holding his arm. He tried to step around her, but she was faster and blocked him. He wrested his arm free. She grabbed it again. Weary of the contest, he stopped.

"Why, Mister Haggard? Tell me why!"

"You know why. He helped to kill my wife."

"He didn't shoot her. Larramore did."

"All you know is what he told you."

"I know *him*, and I know he told the truth."

"Whoever actually fired the shot, they were all responsible. They all killed her. They'll all pay."

"He had mercy on *you*. Won't you have mercy on him?"

Haggard frowned. "*He* had mercy on *me?*"

"Speck Quitman tried to kill you. Johnny stopped him. He knew you meant to kill him, but he wouldn't let Speck kill you. He even took the bullet out of you." Haggard made no reply. She argued, "And he left every cent he had with the Whitakers to pay a doctor to take care of you."

"I didn't accept it. I paid my own way."

"But he *tried*. That's important, isn't it? He tried."

Grimly Haggard said, "Would his money buy my wife back to life? She's dead. Nothing he has done since will change that."

"Will his dying change it?"

He held silent a moment, wanting to say something but not knowing what. "Miss, I'm sorry for you, but there's nothing I can do. There's a blood debt to settle. I'm goin' to see that it's paid!"

He glanced at her face again, and he saw that her terror was gone. In its place was a stiff anger, and perhaps even hatred. "You know what you are, Haggard?" She had dropped the *mister*. "You're a killer. You're a lawman because that makes it legal for you, but if you couldn't be a lawman you'd be an outlaw. You won't listen to reason because you *have* no reason. You're like an animal; it's your nature to kill. It's a disease with you.

"You pretend you're doing this out of love for your wife, but you're lying to us, and you may even be lying to yourself. You've hunted men so long it's turned you into some kind of a wolf. Maybe it's better for her that she *is* dead. She couldn't have lived with you very long. In your own way, you'd have killed her yourself!"

Anger rushed to his face. He lifted his hand as if to strike her, but he stopped himself.

"Go ahead," she taunted him, "hit me. Shoot me, even. If you've got to kill somebody, maybe *I'll* do."

Abruptly he turned away from her. She shouted, "I swear to you, Haggard, if you kill Johnny I'll see you *dead!* Then who'll kill *me?* Where will it ever end?"

Thunder rolled in the distance. Haggard wished it were louder. He walked on, wishing he couldn't hear her, wishing he couldn't feel the stinging lash of her hatred.

Tessie stood in the middle of the street with her small fists clenched and watched Haggard walk stolidly toward the barn. Dugan Whitaker came up from behind and put his hand on her shoulder. "You can't reason with him, girl. I'm afraid the only way anybody could stop him now would be to kill him."

"Uncle Dugan, maybe *you* . . ."

"Could kill him?" He shook his head. "Tessie, I'd do almost anything for you. But that is one thing I couldn't do."

"I didn't mean that. But we've got to warn Johnny."

"It's a long ride to Horsehead. Our buckboard couldn't get there before Haggard and his horse."

"But a horseback rider might, if he was desperate enough."

"Honey, I'm old. There was a time, but I'm not that tough anymore. Haggard would outlast me and outrun me."

"*I'm* young, and I'm desperate enough."

"*You?*" His face furrowed. "It's a hard trip for a girl."

"I've been here three months. I've learned aplenty, and I've toughened a lot. I've got a good reason to make this ride. A better reason than Haggard has."

Doubt hovered in Dugan Whitaker's narrowed eyes. But there was also understanding. "You won't make it, girl. But you'll regret it all your life if you don't make the try. Come on, I know where I can get you a horse." He frowned. "But what if you *do* make it? Even if you do warn Johnny and he runs, what then? Haggard will keep on comin'. He won't stop."

"Then *we'll* keep running, Johnny and me. I should have gone with him before. I'll stay with him this time."

"That's no life, a-runnin'."

"It's better than dying. We'll live while we can."

XIII

Mean enough even in normal times, the Pecos River was on an angry rise. Sodden gray clouds loomed heavy to the north and west. A light mist enveloped this desolate greasewood barren which stretched outward in all directions from Horsehead Crossing.

Johnny Frisco stirred a glowing cowchip fire and put on a smoke-blackened can to boil a mixture of ground coffee and brackish Pecos River water. He reached under a tarp for a couple of dry chips out of a pile which he and Speck had gathered yesterday before the rain started. Chips were about the only fuel here fit to use—"prairie coal," some called them. A man could start a fire with dead greasewood, but it burned too quickly to cook with. Other campers at the crossing had long since used up any dead brush which may have stood along the river.

Speck Quitman rolled his blankets and frowned up at the low-hanging clouds. "Johnny, ain't that girl ever goin' to get here? This is the spookiest place I was ever at."

They had been here three days. Johnny was getting tired of it too. "I told you twenty times, Speck, the letter may have got held up. Not much tellin' when that Mexican got to a post office to mail it."

Speck had changed during the three months or so they had worked on that ranch way down south along the Pecos. He didn't eat much, and he didn't sleep. He smoked up all the tobacco he could get his hands on, and those hands were unsteady. Always when the work would lag a moment, Speck's gaze would lift to the horizon, and fear clouded his eyes.

He had run out of talk a long time ago.

Watching steam start rising from the can, Johnny wished they had been able to fetch along a wagon instead of depending on Tessie to bring hers. A-horseback they hadn't been able to carry much camping equipment. For one thing, he wished they had a barrel so they could fill it and let the water settle before they used it. The flooded river was carrying a lot of mud.

It hadn't tasted very good even before. Now it was about all a man's stomach could stand.

Horsehead Crossing wasn't a pleasant place to camp anyway. There was no shelter. From here back to Castle Gap, all Johnny could see was waist-high greasewood and a scattering of tall Spanish Daggers that had a worrisome way of looking like men, especially in the twilight or in a thin mist like this. He had thought at first Speck was going to come unwound here. Twenty times Speck had sworn he saw one of the daggers move, that it was Milam Haggard. Johnny hadn't wanted to bring Speck here in the first place, but Speck wouldn't have stayed on that ranch without Johnny for all the silver coin west of the Conchos.

Johnny felt an ominous presence about this place, a vague but unmistakable sense of death. For three hundred years white men had known this crossing and had used it—Spaniards first, then the Mexicans and finally the Americans. Indians had swum across here for countless centuries before that. No one knew how many men had died within a stone's throw of this spot. Johnny had found a number of graves along the trail, some of them marked, some of them not. The Pecos was deep and usually swift. Many of the men buried here had underestimated the river.

Then, too, there had been the Indians. Until twenty years or so ago, the fearsome Comanches had haunted this forsaken region. Warfare to them had been a game, though a bloody one. The Comanche War Trail to Mexico had led across here. Only God knew how many captive Mexican women and children had been dragged here in hopeless captivity. No telling how many horses and cattle the Comanches had taken here, or how many scalps. A man halfway across the river made a helpless target.

Bleached bones of horses and cattle told a silent story of hardship and death. They set the mood for this lonesome place, and a cheerless mood it was.

Even as men had used this crossing, they had cursed it.

Speck looked into the steaming can and found to his disappointment that the coffee wasn't ready. He looked eastward again, his face drawn and listless. Then he stiffened. "Johnny, I see somebody comin'."

Johnny glanced up a moment and then said crisply, "Speck, there isn't anybody comin'. Will you ever quit seein' things?"

Speck narrowed his eyes, still peering worriedly through the mist. "I'd of swore . . ." His face was grave. "He's a-comin' though, Johnny. Milam Haggard is comin'. I can feel it in my bones."

"Speck, you've felt Milam Haggard in your bones ever since that mornin' on the Sonora road. There hasn't been a day you haven't looked for him to come."

Speck shivered, and not altogether from the damp air. "There hasn't been an *hour*!" He squatted on his heels and stared eastward, not satisfied that he had been wrong.

Watching him, Johnny felt a touch of pity. Sure, *he* had worried too, but not like Speck. Haggard had become an obsession with him. It seemed the farther they got away from Haggard, the more certain Speck became that they would be found.

Speck poured coffee into a tin cup and sucked his fingers to ease the burn he had taken from the hot can. "Johnny, what if Haggard does come? We ain't even got a gun."

"He lost us, Speck. He's got no idea where we're at. Besides, what would we do with a gun if we had it? We're not goin' to shoot him, not again."

"*I* would. If he was to die, we could live. As long as he lives he's hangin' over our heads like them clouds up there. I'd've killed him that other time if you'd left me alone."

Johnny had argued this out with Speck a hundred times. But nothing was ever final with Speck. Whatever was dwelling on his mind, he always came back to it, picking over the cold bones again and again. "And then what, Speck? He was right; we were wrong. Instead of *him* comin' after us alone, there'd have been a hundred or two of them, and we'd of been dead now instead of sittin' here at Horsehead."

"Might be better dead than to live the way we do, afraid every time we see a stranger. Seein' him all day and *her* all night."

Sadly Johnny shrugged. "Speck, I wish I knew what to tell you."

Speck kept watching the horizon. At length he pushed to his feet excitedly, dropping his cup and splashing coffee out onto the wet ground. "Johnny, it *is* somebody. Look!"

Johnny squinted. Speck was right. Yonder came a rider.

Speck blurted, "It's *him*; it's got to be. Let's saddle up and skin out of here!"

"Be sensible for once, Speck. It won't be Haggard. How could he know?"

"He just knows, that's all. He ain't human."

"He's human enough to get himself shot." But arguing with Speck was as fruitless as talking to that stack of cowchips under the tarp. Speck grabbed up his saddle, blanket and bridle and hurried out to where his horse was picketed. Johnny watched him throw the rig up onto the horse's back.

"Speck, even if it *was* Haggard, where would you go?"

"I'd head out across that river."

"It's too high. You couldn't swim it."

"With *him* after me I could swim the Mississippi."

Johnny gave up arguing. Time was when he could talk sense to Speck, now and again. Lately he couldn't reach him at all. Johnny turned to watch the oncoming rider. Something about the horseman struck him oddly.

"It's a woman, Speck. She's a-ridin' sidesaddle." The rider came nearer. Johnny exclaimed, "Speck, it's Tessie. It's Tessie!"

Speck had just finished tightening the cinch. With relief he said, "High time she was gettin' here. Only, where's her wagon?"

Johnny trotted out afoot to meet her. Recognizing him, she called his name. Johnny reached up for her and brought her down from the saddle and crushed her in his arms. "Tessie, we'd all but given you up. But why did you come by yourself?"

Her voice was urgent. "We've got no time to talk. Milam Haggard's on his way."

His stomach went cold. "Haggard?"

"He got hold of your letter, Johnny. I've ridden as hard as I could to get ahead of him. I passed him in the gap. And he knows it."

Speck had heard. His face drained. "Johnny, I told you I felt it. He's comin'." His voice cracked. "He's comin', and we're goin' to die!"

Johnny spoke impatiently, "Speck, hush up that kind of talk. We got to think."

"It's too late for that. You do what you want to. Me, I'm high-tailin' it across that river. It's still on the rise. Time he gets here maybe he won't be able to follow me."

"It's already too late, Speck. Water's too high."

"With the river we got a chance. With Haggard we got none atall."

Speck swung into the saddle and touched spurs to the bay horse.

Johnny stared after him, not quite believing. "Speck, have you gone plumb crazy? You come back here!"

Speck kept riding.

"Speck," Johnny called anxiously, "if you've got the sense God gave a jackrabbit you'll come back here!" He ran after Speck afoot. Speck saw that Johnny intended to stop him. He spurred again, putting the horse into a long trot. As Speck looked back, Johnny caught a glimpse of his friend's fearstricken face. "Speck, for God's sake stop!"

For an instant Johnny remembered what his father had once said about Speck: *Sometimes he doesn't make good sense. He'll pull a fool stunt and kill himself someday.*

Speck spurred down the wet bank. The bay balked at going into the swirling brown water. Speck kept jabbing him with his spurs and slapping the horse's rump with his hat. Finally the bay jumped off into the river. For a moment it looked as if they were going to be all right. Speck had swum rivers before. Getting out into the fast current, he slipped out of the saddle to give the horse a better chance. He clung to the horn and the saddlestrings.

Something happened. The horse panicked and began threshing. Somehow Speck lost his hold.

Johnny watched openmouthed from the bank. "Tessie," he shouted, "bring my rope. It's on my saddle."

Tessie jerked the hornstring loose and came running with the rope. Meeting her, Johnny grabbed it and ran down the riverbank, stumbling, rolling, regaining his feet.

"Speck! Over here! I got a rope!"

Speck's arms windmilled wildly. Foamy water swirled around him, carrying him swiftly down the river. He saw Johnny and raised his hand. Johnny swung the loop and sent it sailing. But just as it touched the water, Speck went under. When the cowboy came up again, he had missed the rope.

Desperately Johnny re-coiled it and went running again, racing the current. A second time he threw the rope. This time Speck clutched it, and for a moment Johnny thought he had him. But Speck lost his hold. Once more he disappeared beneath the muddy water.

Johnny went running again. This time he knew Speck wouldn't have strength left to hold the rope. Johnny ran until he was sure he was ahead of him. He dropped down over the slippery riverbank, pulling the loop tightly around his own waist and quickly half-hitching the other end of the rope to a salt-cedar. Catching a glimpse of Speck above him, Johnny plunged into the water.

He had no idea the flood could pull so hard. It seemed a futile fight against the swift current, but somehow he made it out into the river. The muddy, salty water burned his eyes, and it was hard for him to see. But he glimpsed Speck almost upon him. He grabbed an arm. "Speck . . ." Water filled his mouth and choked him. He pulled Speck up against him and began trying to fight the current with one arm. It was a hopeless fight. He felt himself going under. But stubbornly he held on to Speck.

He reached the end of the rope. The current pulled him so hard it felt as if the rope would cut him in two. But he kept fighting, and slowly the drag of the current against the rope drew him back toward the bank. He threshed desperately with his free arm. He choked on the bad water, but finally he felt his feet touch bottom. With all the strength that was left in him, he fought his way to the bank.

Tessie was there, wet from the rain, muddy from climbing down the steep bank. She grabbed Johnny's free arm and helped him pull up. He dragged Speck after him. Breathing hard, his heart pounding from exhaustion, Johnny pulled Speck up over the bank and out onto flat ground. Still choking, he turned Speck over onto his stomach and started trying to squeeze the water out of him.

"Here, Johnny," Tessie said, "you're done in. I'll try."

Speck's horse climbed up onto the bank and stood exhausted, hanging its head.

Tessie pumped awhile, till Johnny got over his coughing and regained his breath. Then he tried it. He was getting no response. His heartbeat quickened, and desperation began taking hold of him. "Speck," he cried, half under his breath, "you got to come out of it. Speck!"

But Speck never stirred. Tessie reached for Speck's wrist and felt for a pulse. When she looked up her face was stricken. "Johnny, there's nothing more we can do."

Johnny had sensed it. Now tears came in a blinding rush, burning his eyes. "I tried. Speck, I tried." His throat went tight. He sat on the wet ground, his knees drawn up, his face buried in his arms. Tessie's hand was light and comforting on his shoulder.

After a long time Tessie's voice came soberly, "Johnny, I see a rider coming. It'll be Haggard."

Johnny slowly raised his head and blinked, clearing his eyes. The mist had almost stopped. He could see the tall rider pausing in camp, studying their tracks. In a moment the rider saw them. He reined the horse gently around and came on in a walk, following the river. Across his lap he held a saddlegun.

Tessie bit her lip. "Johnny, what're we goin' to do?"

Johnny clenched his fist. "Earlier, I'd have run." He glanced at Speck. "Now I don't feel like runnin' anymore. I'm tired of runnin'."

"Johnny, I've got a gun. Dugan Whitaker gave it to me."

"No gun, Tessie. Whatever happens, I don't aim to fight him. We were in the wrong."

"But now *he's* in the wrong. He told us himself: they wouldn't even give him a warrant. The law isn't looking for you. Only Haggard is."

Johnny looked sadly at Speck Quitman lying still and silent in the mud. "I wish I'd known that before."

"But don't you see, Johnny? You've got a right to defend yourself now. He's already killed Larramore. In a way, he killed Speck. Now you've got to kill *him* before he kills you."

Johnny shook his head and pushed to his feet. "No, Tessie. I won't kill him."

"Then run, Johnny! Take Speck's horse and run!"

"How far could I get? I've run too long already, and for nothin'. I'm through runnin'. I'm going to stand and face him. Whatever is goin' to happen, let it happen here. Let this be the end of it."

He turned and waited for Haggard.

Milam Haggard had camped in the gap, figuring on riding down to the Pecos crossing in the early hours of morning. He knew the two he sought were down there, for he had seen a pinpoint of firelight. He could have ridden on down and finished it in the night, but he didn't trust himself. He was tired, and the shoulder was still bothering him some. A man could make a mistake in a situation like that, when he wasn't at his best. Better to wait and rest a few hours. He would be ready in the early morning. They would not. That was the time to take them, when there was still sleep in their eyes.

This, then, was the hour he had waited for. This was the final reckoning, when all debts would be paid and the slate wiped clean, when the burden of vengeance at last would be lifted from his shoulders. It had become an oppression of late, as painful as the slow-healing wound that had bent him. He was weary of it. He would be glad when this was over and he could go home—home to the ranch. He would be glad when he no longer had to call up a mental image of Cora's face to keep driving him on.

He had been aware of someone riding far behind him yesterday, but he hadn't thought much of it. People still used this old Butterfield Trail. He hadn't even considered the girl until he saw her ride through the gap and past him this morning. Daylight had not yet come, and he would not even have seen her had she not ridden within fifty feet of his camp. She had been unaware of him until about the same time he had seen her. She had moved into a lope. He had considered saddling up and racing her to the crossing, but she had a good start on him. He would wear out his horse and maybe himself as well.

Let her go, then. He had lost the element of surprise, and he regretted that. But they couldn't go far. He had an idea the river would be up, from the looks of the heavy clouds to the north. So he would catch them soon. Sure, it was two to one, but they were only cowboys. They knew horses and cattle and ropes, but *he* was the one who knew guns. He wouldn't give them a chance to ambush him again.

"It's almost over now, Cora," he spoke aloud. "In a little while you can rest easy."

But he thought of the girl riding far ahead, and he remembered the bitter words she had flung at him in the settlement.

Who is going to rest easy? he asked himself. *Will it be Cora, or me?*

A killer, Tessie Barnett had called him.

Maybe it's better for your wife that she is dead, the girl had shouted. *She couldn't have lived with you very long. In your own way, you'd have killed her yourself.*

"It's not true, Cora," Haggard said. "We'd have had a good life. I'd have changed, for *you*."

He had been sure he could do it. Well, almost sure. But Cora had died, and he *hadn't* changed. That much, at least, he granted the girl.

Certainly he had killed, but always for the right. He had never killed a man who didn't deserve to die, and he had never killed a man who didn't have a chance. He had killed, but he had never murdered. Of that, he was proud.

Moving toward the crossing, he reached down and drew the saddlegun from its scabbard beneath his leg. He brought it up in front of him and rode with sharp eyes watching through the thin mist. He had let these men shoot him once. He wouldn't make that mistake again. The air was wet and chill and he hunched his shoulders, wishing he had brought a coat or a jumper. But perhaps all the chill wasn't from the weather. He sensed death about this miserable place. His eyes were drawn to two unmarked mounds at the side of the hoof-worn trail. The toll of Horsehead Crossing.

Today there would be new graves.

He thought of the cowboys as he had seen them that day on the Sonora road. They were young. They hadn't meant to kill Cora. But she had died. Had it not been for them, she would still live.

Young, they were, and fated to grow no older.

Well, he had seen even younger ones die, young men who had more right to life than these, men who had done no wrong.

He saw the camp ahead, the chips aglow in the shallow firepit. He saw a horse picketed, no saddle on its back, and another horse standing with a sidesaddle. He saw tracks where a third horse had gone down to the river. There were boot tracks too.

At first he figured they were huddled down behind the riverbank, waiting to ambush him. His hand tightened on the short rifle.

Downriver he saw a movement. He made out the girl standing there, and beside her a man sitting on the ground. Watching them cautiously, he reined gently around and moved in their direction. He wondered where the second cowboy was, and the hair stiffened at the back of his neck. He considered the probability that they were trying to lure him into a trap. But presently he saw the body lying at the girl's feet. He saw a bay horse standing on the riverbank, head down, water dripping.

He thought he could guess what had happened.

Rifle ready, he rode on slowly and drew rein twenty feet from Johnny Fristo and Tessie Barnett. He looked down a moment at Speck Quitman.

Johnny Fristo said with an acid bitterness, "Yes, he's dead, Mister Haggard. You wanted to kill him, and you did."

"*I* killed him?"

"With fear. The fear of you drove him to it. So carve another notch on your gun. The credit belongs to you. Enjoy it."

Haggard's mouth tightened. For a moment he felt cheated. Then he knew relief of a kind, for in his mind this had been a just way. "Now there's only you left, Fristo."

Fristo stepped away from the frightened girl. He said flatly, "I'm here."

Haggard frowned. "I don't see your gun."

"I haven't got a gun. Never did have one."

Haggard's eyes narrowed. He hadn't considered this possibility. He nodded toward the body. "Then your friend had one. Get it. I'll give you that much time."

Johnny held still. "He doesn't have one, either."

Haggard eased down from the saddle, keeping the rifle ready, pointed toward Fristo. "He *had* one. He shot me."

"I smashed the rifle. He hasn't had one since."

Haggard stepped away from the horse, frowning. "I've never shot an unarmed man."

"If you shoot me, that's the way it's goin' to have to be."

Haggard's hands flexed nervously on the saddlegun.

Somehow he found himself on the defensive here in a way that puzzled him. Few times in his life had he ever wondered what he should do; he always seemed to know. Now he faced indecision, and it was hard to cope with.

Tessie Barnett said, "Mister Haggard, you killed Larramore. You killed Speck Quitman. Aren't two men enough to pay for what happened to your wife, especially when it was an accident in the first place? How much more blood is it going to take?"

Haggard did not look at her. He kept his eyes on Johnny Fristo as he answered her, for he was not completely convinced that Fristo did not have a gun. "This one is still left. I've never hunted a man in my life that I didn't finally get him."

"Is it your wife you're really thinking of, Mister Haggard?" she demanded. "Or is it yourself?"

He did not reply.

Tessie said bitterly, "Two men dead, and you're fixing to murder another. Wouldn't your wife be proud of you now?"

Haggard tried not to listen. He reached across with his left hand and drew the pistol from the holster on his right hip. "Here, Fristo." He pitched the pistol to Johnny's feet. "Now you've got a gun."

Johnny Fristo never looked at it. "If you want me dead, you'll have to shoot me like I am. I'll not fight you."

Haggard's teeth clamped tightly. He *had* to finish this thing, had to get it behind him forever. But he couldn't just shoot down a man who wouldn't fight back. "I'll trail you. I'll hound you till one day I catch you with a gun!"

"You'll never catch me with one. I intend to never

touch one as long as I live." Johnny's voice tightened. "Mister Haggard, I've lived in hell ever since that day your wife died. I've run from you, and I've died a thousand times. Ever since it happened I've been lookin' back over my shoulder, expectin' to see you come ridin' over a hill to kill me. And when I haven't seen *you* I've seen your wife. Now all of a sudden I'm more tired of runnin' than I am scared of dyin'.

"You want to kill me? Then do it right now, right here. If you don't kill me I'm goin' home where I belong. I'm goin' to tell the world what I've done and learn to live in spite of it. I'm through runnin', and I'm through bein' scared. So shoot me if you want to. But if you're ever goin' to do it, do it now!"

He waited a moment for Haggard to move. Then he turned his back and started walking slowly toward Speck Quitman's bay horse.

Haggard brought up the rifle. "Fristo, stop!"

Tessie cried, "No, Mister Haggard. If you shoot him now it'll be murder. I'll tell them all how it was. You won't be the hunter then. They'll be huntin' *you*!"

Haggard didn't want to do it this way, but a desperation was driving him. "Fristo, for God's sake turn and face me! Don't make me shoot you in the back!" He wanted to get it over with. He felt a revulsion against himself even as he aimed the rifle at Johnny Fristo's back. But he had to end it now.

From the corner of his eye he saw Tessie Barnett reach into her jacket. He heard the click of a hammer.

What Haggard did then was pure reflex. He swung the rifle toward the girl. In horror he realized what he was doing, but he was unable to stop the motion he had started. It was lightning swift and automatic. He tried to force himself to raise the muzzle as he squeezed the trigger. The saddlegun roared. The butt of it jarred his shoulder, sending a sharp pain slashing through the old wound.

He heard himself cry out in disbelief even before he lowered the rifle. He froze, horrified at what he had done.

The pistol dropped from the girl's hand. She stared at him in wide-eyed surprise, the color suddenly wiped out of her face. Her left hand lifted toward her shoulder, and she gasped.

Johnny Fristo shouted, "Tessie!" He took two long strides and grabbed her as she started to sag. "Tessie!"

Haggard came out of his shock. He threw the saddlegun away and stepped toward the girl. "My God! Oh my God!" Blood began to spread through the shoulder of her jacket. "I didn't mean to, girl. I couldn't stop it. I tried to raise the muzzle."

Ashen-faced, Johnny Fristo was easing her to the ground.

Haggard tried to get control of himself. "I didn't mean to. It was an accident."

He realized then how futile that sounded, and where he had heard it before. He put his hand over his face.

In a moment Johnny Fristo said husky-voiced, "It isn't so bad, Mister Haggard. You *did* raise that muzzle. You just kind of grazed her."

Haggard swayed. "I thought I'd killed her." He rubbed his hand over his face again. "How could I have lived with myself?"

Johnny Fristo held the girl tightly in his arms, relief in his eyes. In a little while he said, "Maybe you'd have learned—the way *I've* had to learn."

Reaction nearly got the best of Haggard then. He trembled in realization of what he had almost done.

He had almost murdered a man. Had it not been for the girl, he would have shot Johnny Fristo in the back. And then he had almost killed the girl.

Cora, I meant it for you! All that I've done has been for you!

"Fristo," he said finally, "we'd better do something about that wound of hers. She's going to be sick."

Johnny Fristo's voice was tight and grim. "I reckon I can take care of her, Mister Haggard. If you've finished your business here, maybe you'd better just go."

Haggard flinched. Then, "Yes, I guess I'm finished."

He glanced at Speck Quitman lying on the muddy ground, and he looked once more at the girl. "I'm finished." He turned toward his horse. He thought of his pistol lying on the ground where he had tossed it at Fristo's feet. He thought of the smoking saddlegun he had dropped.

But he did not pause to pick them up. He hoped he never had to look at another gun.

Swinging into the saddle, he gave one quick glance to the violent Horsehead Crossing, then reined his horse eastward toward the cleft that was Castle Gap. His shoulders were bent, and his head was down.

He never looked back.

Turn the page for a preview of

Many A River

Elmer Kelton

Available now

A FORGE HARDCOVER

ISBN-13: 978-0-7653-2050-6   ISBN-10: 0-7653-2050-9

I

North Texas, 1855

Jeffrey Barfield wondered how much farther Papa would continue to travel before he found a settle-down place that suited him. The family had left Arkansas by wagon two months ago and slowly picked their way across the eastern part of Texas, looking for land Papa would consider to be just right. Mama had seen a dozen sites she would be happy with, but Papa invariably said, "There's bound to be better a little farther west."

Eight-going-on-nine, Jeffrey was beginning to fear the family would still be wandering when he celebrated his next birthday. They had passed through Fort Worth, then moved on westward, stopping hopefully here a day, there a day, and going on. Now they had camped on a pleasant, clear-running creek miles beyond Weatherford. Papa walked in a slow circle, kicking up soil with his boot, then reaching down with calloused farmer hands to scoop up a bit of it. He sniffed at it and let it slowly spill out between his fingers.

Watching from afar, Jeffrey said, "Reckon this is it, Mama? Reckon he'll decide this is the place?"

Mama touched his shoulder gently. She looked tired. "I don't know, son. I've wished so many times . . ." She turned toward her campfire. "You'd better fetch me a little more dry wood."

Jeffrey heard a boyish shout and glanced about for his younger brother. Todd was romping with a brown dog that had accompanied the family as the wagon bumped its way through Arkansas. With a fleeting impatience, Jeffrey shouted, "Hush up, Todd. You'll run off any game that's within hearin' of you."

Todd quieted down for a minute or two but quickly forgot Jeffrey's admonition. He began playing fetch-the-stick with the dog. Jeffrey shrugged. Remaining quiet seemed too much to ask of an energetic five-year-old boy.

He gathered a few small branches from dead brush and broke them across his knee, carrying them back to the fire. Papa had strayed three hundred yards from the wagon. Mama raised her hand to her slat bonnet to shade her eyes from the noonday sun. She said, "Better go fetch him, son. Dinner'll be ready when you-all get back."

"Yes, ma'am. Papa loses all track of time."

He met Todd walking in from his game. Not seeing the dog, he asked, "Where's Brownie?"

"He got tired of chasin' a stick. He took off after a rabbit."

"You better get back to the wagon and wash your face and hands. It'll soon be time to eat."

Todd quickened his pace. He liked to play, but eating pleased him even more.

Jeffrey gave Papa the message. Papa sounded disappointed. "All right, I'm done here. Soon as we've finished eatin' dinner, we'll break camp and move on."

Jeffrey tried not to frown. Mama always said Papa knew best, even when she didn't believe it herself. "This isn't the place?"

"Maybe a little farther on."

They had not seen a soul since they left Weatherford. Jeffrey asked, "Ain't we gotten out pretty far past everybody else?"

"That's the way I like it. We get first pick."

At the wagon, Papa broke the news that they were moving on. Mama took it without comment, but Todd protested, "Brownie ain't come back. We can't just leave him."

Papa said, "If he don't find his way to us, we'll have to go without him."

Todd puckered up. Papa said sternly, "You're too big to start cryin'."

Todd said, "I don't ever cry."

Jeffrey saw the hurt in his brother's eyes. He said, "I'll go hunt for him. He may not have sense enough to follow us."

Papa warned, "Don't waste much time. We'll be startin' pretty soon."

The noonday sun bore heavily on Jeffrey's thin shoulders and sent sweat trickling down his freckled face. He never cussed in front of Papa or Mama, but he was a mile or more from them now. He stated his opinion of the wayward dog in terms he had heard his father use in addressing a team of mules. Papa often relied on profanity for its ability to relieve stress.

"You can stay out here and starve to death for all I care," Jeffrey shouted at the absent animal.

Well, no big loss. Brownie rarely played with him, preferring to rip around with Todd. Jeffrey turned and started back, his feet dragging, his steps shorter than when he had begun. He had not gone far before he heard the dog barking off to his left. He saw a moving cloud of dust and heard the drumming of hooves. Someone was pushing a band of horses in a slow lope. As wind shifted the dust, he counted a dozen or more riders.

He froze in midstride. They were Indians, and they were riding headlong toward the wagon camp.

The shock gave Jeffrey fresh strength. He broke into a run, shouting a warning. His was a boy's voice, high-pitched and too weak to carry far. Remembering terrible tales he had heard about Indian raids, he began crying. He heard a shot and recognized the sound of the rifle. Papa was serving notice that he intended to defend himself and his family.

Several Indians left the horse herd and circled the wagon. Papa's rifle fired once more, then a shotgun blasted. That would be Mama, pitching in. Jeffrey was close enough now to see Papa go down and to hear Mama scream before a warrior crushed her head with a club.

He realized that the Indians could see him if they looked in his direction. He dropped to his stomach and hid himself in the tall grass. Instinct cried out for him to rush to the wagon and try to help, but fear paralyzed him. An inner voice told him it was already too late, that he would only get himself killed.

He heard Todd cry out as an Indian lifted him onto his horse. The boy futilely beat the warrior with his fists. The man swung the hard handle of a rawhide quirt and struck Todd a sharp blow to the side of his head. Todd went limp. Jeffrey then lost sight of his brother and the Indian in the stirring of dust as warriors circled the wagon. He heard them shouting in celebration while they looted it of blankets and foodstuffs. They gathered up the mule team Papa had staked on grass near camp and tried to set fire to the wagon. They succeeded only in burning much of the canvas cover before wind snuffed out the blaze. They rode away, adding the mules to their band of loose horses.

Jeffrey lay on the ground for several minutes, trembling, fearing that some Indians might lag behind and see him. Finally, choking with fear, he forced himself to his feet and trudged to the wagon. He knew what he would surely find, but he denied it to himself. Mama and Papa must somehow have survived. They had to.

But they had not. Mama lay twisted on the ground, eyes open but not seeing. Her head was bloody, her scalp torn away. Wind tugged at her long skirt. Papa lay across a hot cast-iron dutch oven that sat atop live coals. His clothing smoldered, and Jeffrey smelled burning flesh. Papa too had been scalped.

Todd was not there.

Jeffrey dragged his father away from the heat and used his bare hands to beat out the slow flames that had burned holes in shirt and trousers. He dropped to his knees and let the tears flow. Body quaking, he shouted out in grief and fear and rage.

He lost all sense of time, crying until he was exhausted. Eventually he forced himself to his feet and began to look around, to take stock of the situation into which he had so suddenly been thrust. Mama and Papa were dead. Todd was gone, probably dead too, or he would be when the Indians grew tired of him. Of what use could a five-year-old boy be to them?

Flies had already found his parents' wounds. Mama had been wearing an apron. Jeffrey spread it to cover her head. He found Papa's fallen hat and laid it across his father's still face.

He knew there was no need to look for the rifle or the shotgun. The Indians would have taken those as prizes of the raid. He thought of the dog. It had barked at the horses, probably alerting the Indians to the wagon camp even before they saw it. Jeffrey ventured out, calling again for Brownie.

He found the dog a hundred yards away, dead, with two large wounds in its side. A third wound still had part of an arrow shaft in it. Evidently the Indians had tried to retrieve their arrows but had broken one off.

"Damn you, Brownie," Jeffrey said, "you had it comin' to you."

He realized then that his own life had been spared because the dog had wandered off. Otherwise he would have been in camp when the Indians struck. He moderated his tone. "I hope you caught your rabbit."

The family milk cow had been staked near the wagon. She lay dead, a hind leg cut off and carried away. It had been one of Jeffrey's chores to milk her twice a day. She was mean about kicking, so he did not mourn her.

Jeffrey could not bear to see Mama and Papa lying there on the ground. They needed to be buried. He found the shovel where it was supposed to be, strapped to the side of the wagon. The Indians had seen no need for it. He was practiced in use of the shovel. He had dug fire pits and unearthed old stumps to serve as firewood for his mother as they had moved west from Arkansas. He chose a piece of ground above the creek's high-water mark and began to dig a hole wide enough that he could bury Papa and Mama side by side, the way they had been as far back as he could remember.

The grave was waist deep when he heard horses. Fear fell over him again like a smothering blanket. He dropped to his stomach in the hole, certain more Indians were coming. He heard the horses stop at the camp. As men raised their voices in excitement, he recognized familiar words. These riders were not Indians. Climbing out of the hole, he waved his hat over his head, afraid the men might ride on without seeing him. He began running, stumbling toward the wagon, trying to shout but not finding his voice.

A couple of men raised rifles, startled by the boy's unexpected appearance. They lowered them quickly. One rider moved out to meet him, dismounting and kneeling, anxiously studying Jeffrey at his own eye level. The man was two hundred pounds of muscle and bone. His bearing indicated that he was the kind who would automatically take charge without waiting for someone else. Touching a huge hand to Jeffrey's shoulder, he demanded, "Anybody here besides you?"

"No, sir," Jeffrey managed, his voice breaking. "The Indians didn't see me." Guilt burned deeply as he admitted, "I hid."

"A good thing you did. I suppose that's your mother and father we found back yonder?"

Jeffrey sobbed once, then forced a measure of control. "Yes, sir. And they carried off my little brother." He felt a moment of hope. "Maybe you can catch them and make them give Todd back."

The big man's heavy eyebrows came together in a dark frown. "We're tryin' to catch them, but I doubt it'll do your brother any good. The minute we close with them, they generally kill any prisoners. Best we can hope for is to make them bleed for what they've done. And maybe we can get back the horses they stole on this raid."

Hope collapsed as quickly as it had risen. "You can't save Todd?"

"I'm sorry to put it to you so strong, but if they haven't already killed him, they will."

Jeffrey lost control and wept again. In a kindly voice the bearded man said, "You've got to face it like a man. He's gone, like your mama and daddy are gone."

The other men gathered around, some voicing sympathy, others demanding angrily that they keep riding. They had raiders to catch and kill. The bearded man said, "Adam, how about you and Matthew Temple stayin' here with this boy? The rest of us will see if we can get us some Indians."

Jeffrey said, "I want to go with you. I want to find my brother."

"You'd best put aside any notion of seein' your brother again. It'd just lead to fresh disappointment. You've got hurt enough already."